AFTERMATH: KODIAK & DAWN

Book 1 of the Aftermath Series

by Douglas J. Eboch

Published by SEE EWE Publishing

ISBN: 9798847897198

For Mom & Dad

Chapter 1

A pigeon pecks at the asphalt for crumbs, minding its own business, when…

BLAM!

Someone puts a bullet through the poor bird.

The pigeon bleeds out in the middle of Main Street, the aptly named central thoroughfare of Mt. Tucker. Mt. Tucker is a typical small, Midwestern town – mom and pop stores gradually being replaced by national chains. It's midday, but the place is deserted. The sun shines. A gentle breeze ruffles the green maples shading the wide sidewalks. But no people enjoy the pleasant summer day.

Then the mayor steps out of an alley between the Starbucks and the Baskin Robbins. He's wearing an N95 filter mask, plastic face shield, and rubber gloves that go up to his elbows. He approaches the dead pigeon and picks it up with long, stainless steel tongs.

As he walks down the center of the street, the bird held out in front of him, dozens of townspeople emerge from the stores. They watch the mayor pass the Pizza Hut, H&M, the boarded-up KFC, the Verizon store, and Claire's Mt. Tucker Diner – where Claire herself still grills omelets and burgers in the kitchen and bakes fresh pies from her grandmother's recipes. The mayor reaches the end of the street and steps up to the main gate in the high, razor-wire-topped, chain-link fence that surrounds the town.

Two guards look down from their post in the wooden tower by the main gate, one resting his arm on a mounted fifty-caliber machine gun.

The mayor flings the dead pigeon over the fence. It plops into the long grass on the other side, below a sign that reads:

CLEAN ZONE
NO ADMITTANCE

The mayor steps back. Raises his face shield. He looks up at the fake owls mounted on the corner of every building on Main Street. They're not doing the job of keeping the birds away anymore. Next city council meeting, they'll have to discuss netting the entire town again.

Shane Carpenter takes a swig of coffee and scans the woods bordering the highway. He catches a glimpse of himself in the side mirror of his crimson Peterbilt 579EV big rig. Dark hair tousled. Three-day stubble. Fraying red flannel shirt. He looks old, much older than his thirty-one years. But not as old as he feels.

He adjusts his grip on the steering wheel.

He's part of a convoy. But the trucks in this convoy are all custom altered for defense. Plates of steel welded over wheels. Spikes or barbed wire circling them as if to repel boarders. A gun turret mounted on one cab, a pair of small rockets on the roof of another.

Each has a nickname and logo painted on the door: "Scorpion," "Royal Flush," "The Duchess" – that sort of thing. Similarly modified muscle cars act as outriders.

Shane's rig has a black bear pawprint painted on the door, the name "Kodiak" beneath. That's his handle.

He spots a highway sign:

MT. TUCKER – NEXT EXIT

He picks up his CB handset. "Breaker two-four, Kodiak here. Looks like this is where I part company with you folks. Over."

A husky voice comes over the CB. "La Llorona, here. You keep your eyes open, Kodiak. The Piranhaz have been targeting solo rigs like crazy in this area. Over."

"Don't worry, L. I can take care of myself. Over."

"Yeah, but what fun is that? Over."

The corner of Shane's mouth curls up slightly – about as close to a smile as you're likely to get from him. "Hold that thought, and I'll see you back in Ashford. Out." Shane eases his truck out of the line and onto the transition road.

Shane cruises along the rural highway to Mt. Tucker – two lanes, a ditch on either side, rolling wooded hills beyond. No other vehicles.

A few miles in, the road curves around a fifteen-foot-high granite boulder on his right. Shane makes the turn–

And hits the brakes.

A tree has fallen across the road, right to left. Shane's truck *squeals*, *groans*, and skids to a stop with a few feet to spare.

The tree is uprooted – could be natural. But anybody might be hiding in those woods. He throws the truck into reverse, backs up alongside the boulder.

He grabs his 9 mm semi-automatic pistol from the glove compartment. Climbs out the passenger door. Drops into the muddy ditch between the boulder and the truck, protected from the woods. The scent of pine hangs heavy in the warm, moist air. The woods are quiet. Like the trees are holding their breath.

He retrieves a long, heavy coil of chain from a storage compartment on the side of his cab. Hooks one end of the chain to a battering ram welded to the truck's bumper.

He crawls up the ditch, staying low.

He reaches the tree. The base of the trunk spans the ditch. He tosses the chain over it, hooks the chain around the trunk…

A flash in the woods – reflection off metal – movement!

Shane dives to his belly as–

BLAM – BLAM – BLAM!

–bullets *slam* into the downed tree, showering him with damp splinters.

Ambush.

Shane crawls under the tree, up on the other side. Uses it for cover as he exchanges fire with his attackers, the thunderous *CRACK* of the shots echoing through the still afternoon.

There are at least two on either side of the road. He gets glimpses of them adjusting position in the trees, trying to get vantage.

One of Shane's shots elicits a cry from the opposite woods. He scrambles across the roadway along the downed tree, drops into the ditch on that side of the road.

He peeks up at the truck, fifty long feet away. He begins crawling along the ditch.

RAINBOW

Crouches behind a leafy bush in the woods ten feet from the road. She keeps her head down so her position isn't given away by the spiked mohawk died in rainbow colors from whence she gets her nickname. She wipes her left hand on her leather pants and then grips her AR-5 assault rifle. Her associates are keeping the trucker busy. It's time to move.

She scrambles around the brush. Leaps the ditch, her combat boots splattering in the mud on the other side. Dashes across the asphalt to the truck.

She moves along the big rig, back to front. Slips in through the driver's door.

The engine is off. She tries the ignition button – no luck. The trucker must be too far away for his key fob to connect.

That would have been too easy anyway. She could wait until the others take out the trucker and retrieve the fob from his body, but there's always the chance he could escape now that he's survived their initial attack. Besides, Rainbow's not really the waiting around type. She slides under the dash and pries open a panel to hack the truck's system with the app Malcolm downloaded from the dark web.

Then she notices a corner of carpet curled up under the passenger seat. What have we here? She pulls the carpet back. There's a hidden compartment underneath. She opens the compartment and discovers–

A duffle bag.

She unzips it. There are bundles of cash inside. Tens of thousands of dollars.

Rainbow grins.

Until she hears the *GROWL.*

From the sleeper area – she's looking into the drooling fangs of a dog, a black and brown mutt – part Rottweiler, part wolf, part hell hound.

Rainbow's grin fades.

She eases herself back against the driver side door while at the same time retrieving the AR-5 she left on the seat. The dog doesn't give her much time – lunges–

Rainbow's flailing hand opens the door–

Rainbow, the dog, and the AR-5 tumble out of the cab onto the roadway.

Rainbow fends the dog off with her left arm – the beast tears up that arm pretty good.

Rainbow manages to get leverage – plants a foot in the dog's chest – shoves him away. She dives for the AR-5 – rolls to her feet – aims the gun at the lunging canine–

And then the trucker stands up out of the ditch, pistol leveled–

BLAM!

The trucker's bullet tears into Rainbow's left shoulder – fire explodes down her arm, into her chest. She's thrown back – never gets the chance to pull the trigger.

SHANE

Stomach twists into a knot. The hijacker with the rainbow mohawk almost killed Slaughter. The dog pounces on her now, but there's no time for that.

Shane yells, "Slaughter, *kego*!" Shane has trained his best friend to respond to commands in Ojibway, his tribal language. Few people will be able to guess those words.

Slaughter obediently leaps back inside the cab.

Three of the hijackers – leather and denim clad biker types – scramble from the trees. They open fire as Shane lunges across the road, vaults the moaning, rainbow-mohawked hijacker, leaps into the cab. He pulls the door shut – bullets *SLAM* into the glass–

Thankfully, it's bullet proof.

The bullets bounce away, leaving behind small, opaque, craters in the glass.

Shane starts the truck – shifts into reverse – backs up. The chain does its job. Pulls the downed tree parallel to the road.

The three gangsters run back into the woods.

Shane shifts, drives forward.

In his side mirror he sees the rainbow-mohawked hijacker roll out of the way in time to avoid becoming roadkill.

The truck passes the downed tree, picking up speed. But the chain is still attached, and Shane's not stopping to un-attach it. As the chain reaches its full length, it snaps taut – and now the truck is dragging the tree behind it.

Shane passes a turnout. The three gangsters are there, just climbing onto motorcycles. The motorcycles – battered, customized, gas-powered sports bikes – each have an image of a piranha emblazoned on the gas tank. So, Shane's attackers are members of the Piranhaz gang (they added a Z to show they're keepin' it real).

The gangsters peel out in pursuit.

But they have a difficult time closing because that tree is bouncing behind the speeding truck, whipsawing across the road.

Shane watches in his side mirror as one of the bikers tries to move up on his left. *WHAM* – the gangster is pulverized by the tree, his remains tossed casually into the woods.

A second one tries the other side – and miraculously makes it! (Barely.)

Shane watches the gangster move up along the passenger side of the truck. The truck's tires have armor protecting their sides, but the gangster aims at the right, front tire from behind.

Shane veers left and hits the brakes. The truck drops back behind the bike.

The gangster hits his brakes – and the bike can stop more quickly. He falls back alongside the truck.

But what the poor gangster didn't think about is that tree. It doesn't have brakes. And Shane veered left.

The tree tumbles forward along the right side of the truck – end over end, spraying pine needles and twigs everywhere. The root end comes down–

And crushes the gangster.

The tree bounces back up, leaving a pile of motorcycle parts and gangster parts in a puddle of bodily fluid.

Shane hits the accelerator. One motorcyclist left.

This guy's learned from his buddies' mistakes, though. He jumps the ditch and goes overland – out of range of the slowly disintegrating tree. He moves up driver's side, engine revving in a high-pitched whine.

Shane gets on the CB. "Kodiak to Mt. Tucker, come back."

"Mt. Tucker, go ahead."

"I'm coming in with a parasite. Can you help? Over."

"We've got you. You need to get past the old fruit stand to be in range of our tower. Over."

Shane floors it but the motorcycle keeps pace on the other side of the ditch. The gangster takes some shots with his AR-5 – the truck's armor holds.

Shane lowers the window a few inches, fires a couple rounds with his 9mm through the gap. Nearly impossible to hit the gangster that way, but the bike falls back half a dozen yards just in case.

Shane looks in the mirror. The gangster slings the rifle and pulls a hand grenade from the bike's saddlebag. Uh oh.

But before the gangster can throw the grenade, he must dodge some obstacles on the roadside – a big rock, an old fuel tank–

–and a crumbling wooden fruit stand.

The gangster pulls back alongside Shane's cab. Pulls the grenade pin with his teeth. Cocks his arm to toss it.

CHUK-CHUK-CHUK – he's chewed up by machine gun fire out of nowhere–

–tumbles back off his mangled bike–

–the grenade bounces across the road behind the truck–

KABOOM – the explosion blows the tree in half.

The chain rips off the shattered lumber, drags behind the truck.

Shane shudders. Now that the danger's passed, nausea creeps into his belly. He looks to the guard tower near the gate to Mt. Tucker and gives a little salute to the guards who just saved his life.

Chapter 2

Shane backs his truck up to the Mt. Tucker loading dock. He's not inside the clean zone, but rather in a separate fenced area where the town interfaces with outsiders. One of the guards in the tower watches him from behind the mounted 50mm gun. Those guards just saved Shane's life, but if he made any move to breach the town's perimeter, he knows they wouldn't hesitate to take him out.

Shane makes his living off small clean-zone towns like this. It took longer for the H5N6 flu to reach rural areas, so many of them were able to seal themselves off before anyone got infected. They'd had some practice, too. This was the third pandemic to sweep the country in Shane's lifetime. Everyone thought Covid-19 was a once-in-a-century phenomenon, but it turned out it was just the first in a wave of viruses. Some people blame climate change, others say it's government experiments. Shane's heard crazier theories, but none of it much matters to him. What matters is that this pandemic looks like it may be the one to finally break civilization.

Many of the small clean-zone towns are struggling economically, but Mt. Tucker's clean zone encompasses a cheese factory, and it seems to be thriving based on how often Shane's called to make deliveries here. Of course, the factory depends on milk from farmers outside the clean zone, and many of the farmers who survived this pandemic are being run off by marauders like the Piranhaz, so it's unclear how long the good times will last for Mt. Tucker. But that's not Shane's problem. If there's one thing he's learned in the last four years, it's to take one day at a time.

When the truck is in position at the loading dock, Shane puts on his N95 mask and hops out. He goes to the back of the trailer, unlocks the doors, and stands aside. Only then do townspeople in N95 masks, face shields, and latex gloves emerge from the loading dock to unload his cargo of sealed crates. Meanwhile, Shane detaches the chain from his bumper and coils it back up.

When he finishes that task, he goes to the pay window in the side of the building. The clerk today is Riley. He knows her by her pale blue eyes, heavy with eyeliner and gold mascara. When practically everyone was wearing a facemask all day, elaborate eye makeup became the fashion.

Riley pulls a stack of cash bound with a rubber band from under the counter. "You know, Shane, coming up with this much cash is kind of difficult way out here."

Shane takes his money. "I appreciate the effort."

"I'm just saying, everyone else uses electronic transfer. The banks still function. Better than most things, actually."

Riley's not wrong, but Shane prefers to keep his money close at hand given all the infrastructure that's failed over the last few years. Besides, it's earmarked for a transaction that would be best kept off the record. There's no reason to debate any of that with Riley, though, so Shane says nothing.

Riley sighs. "Here's the dinner you ordered from Claire's. And she made you an apple pie. No charge." She passes Shane a covered to-go dish and a pie wrapped in foil.

Shane grins. "Tell Claire I owe her one. Okay if I overnight in the loading area?"

"Of course."

Dawn Harding removes the hair tie from her ponytail and shakes out her long, blond hair. She's sweaty from soccer practice and the early evening breeze feels good. She bites her lip. She's going to miss soccer. She's also going to miss her long, blond hair. Or at least she's going to miss the jealous looks it elicits from the other girls at the high school.

But she can't think about that now. She skips up the walk to her house.

Her parents sit in identical recliners facing the TV, her dad reading a novel and her mom knitting. They are both in their late forties, a little overweight. Her mom is wearing jeans and a shapeless green sweater;

her dad is wearing cargo pants and a blue polo shirt. They have zero fashion sense. The aroma of pot roast drifts in from the kitchen. One of her dad's favorites.

On TV, a perky talk show host – Katy Smith – interviews Reverend Elliot – resplendent in swept back silver hair and a shiny, powder blue suit.

"How do you respond to criticism of your statement that the pandemic was, 'God's punishment for gay marriage and abortion'?" Katy asks.

"I stand by my words," the Reverend booms. "The pandemic is not a tragedy, rather it is a cleansing, like Noah's flood...."

"How was practice, Sweetie?" Dad asks, without looking up from his book.

"Good," Dawn replies.

"Get cleaned up," Mom says. "Dinner will be ready in an hour."

Dawn pulls off her cleats as Reverend Elliot continues ranting, "...it is vital that the people of God bring morally right values back to this country...."

Mom glances at the TV. "That blouse is a good color for Katy, don't you think, Hon?"

"Mm-hm," Dad murmurs. "Switch it to that celebrity karaoke show, would you?"

Dawn jogs upstairs, peeling off her damp jersey even before she reaches her room. She tosses it in the hamper and removes the rest of her clothes.

The hot shower is luxurious. It may be the last one she has for a while. She lingers over washing her hair, inhaling the lavender scent of her shampoo. Her father is probably fuming downstairs over the waste of water, but she doesn't care.

Sooner or later, though, all good things must end. She gets out of the shower and towels off. She wraps herself in the fluffy towel and hops onto her bed, sitting cross-legged amidst a small army of stuffed animals.

She digs her pink, sticker-covered phone out of her gym bag. There are a dozen texts from her friends. She resists the urge to reply. She needs to leave those mundane concerns behind. Instead, she brings up Eric's number. Types out a text to him:

Leaving now c u soon XOXO

She tosses the phone in a black duffle bag by her desk. Hops off the bed. Steps into her closet.

She puts on her black track suit and pulls on a black wool cap, shoving her damp hair up underneath it. She exits the closet, sits on the bed, and slips her feet into her hiking boots.

She takes a last look around her room. The vision board plastered with inspirational quotes and pictures of European castles. The cardboard finger puppet theater she made in third grade. The fishbowl full of shells she collected on that vacation to Florida way back when. The shelf of soccer and softball trophies and medals. The quilt her grandma made. She's lived her whole life in this room. It's been her refuge, her own little territory, an extension of her psyche, growing and changing as she's grown and changed, but with memories of her childhood everywhere.

Still, once again, all good things must end. It's time to think about her future.

She grabs the duffle bag.

Slides open the window.

Climbs out.

Rainbow parks her motorcycle next to the wooden sign that used to read "Silver River Boy Scout Camp" but now sports a spray-painted Piranhaz logo. Her mangled left arm hangs limply at her side, throbbing. That pain is nothing compared to the burning from the bullet hole in her shoulder, though. She scavenged some cloth from Cisco's shirt to plug the wound – Cisco won't be needing that shirt after getting crushed by the tree – but blood still oozes out and trickles down Rainbow's biceps. She presses on the wound with her right palm despite the nausea it elicits. There will be time to focus on the pain later.

Right now, she's focused on revenge.

She strides to the lodge, slams through the door into the common room.

Gangsters play pool, drink beer, smoke pot, blare tunes, make out. Somewhere across the room, Bones shouts, "And boom, another kill for me. Tyler, if you hide in the tower, I'm gonna grenade your ass every time."

Rainbow ignores the stares of the other Piranhaz, stalks over to the corner where Bones is playing X-Box with Tyler and Mouse.

Bones is the leader of the Piranhaz. He's a big, bald, muscle-bound guy in doctor's scrubs with tattoos of all his bones, from skull to phalanges, across his body.

"Bones," Rainbow growls.

He glances up at her. "What happened to you?"

"Tuck, Willard, and Cisco are dead. Some fucking trucker we were jacking killed them."

Bones' jaw goes tight. He pauses the game and studies her. "A trucker? One, single trucker?"

"He wasn't a normal trucker."

"Oh, I see. He was a super trucker. Or maybe you four are just crappy hijackers."

Rainbow feels her face go hot. Everyone is watching them now.

Big-O, a heavyset Latina with a shaved head, coughs.

Bones turns on her. "Big O. Quarantine."

"I'm not sick!" she protests. "I just smoked a bowl."

"Quarantine," Bones growls.

Big O sighs and stomps off toward the quarantine cabin.

Bones turns back to his game.

"We need to go after him," Rainbow cries. "He was heading to Mt. Tucker; he'll have to come back the same way. He had a bear claw symbol on his truck."

Bones rubs a hand across his bald scalp. "That sounds like a lot of effort for one truck."

"If we let him get away, he'll tell everyone the Piranhaz are pussies!"

Bones spins on her. "You know what would convince people we aren't pussies, Rainbow? If you didn't fuck up in the first place!"

Rainbow tries to cross her arms but her shoulder screams in protest. "Fine. By the way, he was carrying a shitload of cash."

That gets Bones' attention. "Yeah? Define shitload."

"At least a couple hundred thousand."

Bones weighs this information. Then he smiles. "Piranhaz, saddle up. We're going after super trucker."

"When we catch him, he's mine," Rainbow says.

"Fine."

"And his little dog, too."

Chapter 3

Dawn stands six feet from the edge of the chain link fence that's surrounded Mt. Tucker for the last two-and-a-half years. It was originally installed to keep potentially infected people out – a requirement of the Klemper Act, which allowed towns where there were no positive cases of the virus to bar entry to outsiders. More recently, the fence has also protected Mt. Tucker from malignant human intruders.

The fence itself is a dozen feet high and topped by razor wire. This section runs through the woods, out of sight of any of the town buildings, which is why Dawn chose it. But she also knows there are motion sensors that will alert the police to any breach. She could probably escape into the woods even if she tripped the sensors – the cops would be looking for people trying to get *into* Mt. Tucker, after all, not people trying to get away – but she'd rather not take that chance.

That's why she stashed the twenty-foot ladder beside the old maple tree with the long, heavy branches.

She brushes aside some of the leaves she used to cover the ladder, then shakes the rest free. She sets the ladder up under the thick branch that extends out over the fence.

She slings the strap of the duffle bag over her shoulder and climbs up. The ladder doesn't quite reach the branch, but it's easy enough to pull herself up into the tree. She lays on her belly and shimmies out along the branch.

It looks a lot higher from up here. Dawn is getting queasy. Cool sweat trickles down her ribs. But she needs to soldier on. There will be bigger challenges than this beyond the fence.

She passes over the razor wire.

CRACK!

She freezes, her breath coming in quick pants. That was from the tree behind her.

But it seems to be holding. She doesn't have a lot of options. She takes a deep, slow breath and keeps moving, inching out along the branch.

About four feet past the fence, she decides it's time to descend. In her imagination, she was going to go out another six feet, but that cracking sound changed those plans. She should be far enough to avoid the motion sensors… hopefully.

She sits up carefully, straddling the branch. Unzips the duffel halfway and retrieves the rope she put on top. She ties the rope around the branch, using the bowline knot she learned in Scouts, and drops it to the ground.

She pauses, takes another deep breath. Her whole body is trembling.

She grabs the rope in her right hand, left arm wrapped around the branch, and swings her legs off the tree. She wraps her legs around the rope. Moment of truth – how well did she remember that bowline knot?

She releases her grip on the tree and grabs the rope tightly with both hands.

It holds.

Another deep breath.

She shimmies down.

She's a few feet above the ground when there's another *CRACK* from the branch.

She panics and releases the rope – hits the ground with both feet in a crouch, but falls back, landing painfully on her butt.

She's down.

Outside the fence.

The fence that's protected her from disease and who knows what else. It's been over three years since she last left Mt. Tucker. And now she can never go back.

But that was the plan. She gets to her feet.

She considers the rope dangling from the branch. Somebody could use that to climb up to the tree and crawl across the branch to get inside the fence. She can't leave a security risk like that behind. She finds a foot-long, heavy hunk of wood. Ties it to the end of the rope. Hurls it up into the air.

It takes her three tries, but she finally gets the piece of wood to go over the branch. The rope catches on the bark as the wood hunk falls back down, bringing it to a stop ten feet in the air. That should keep anyone from getting in easily.

Including Dawn. She has no choice now.

She adjusts the duffel on her shoulder and heads into the woods, toward her new life.

The sleeper area in the back of Shane's cab is small but comfortable. Postcards, maps, a calendar, and sports team flags cover the walls, mini-fridge, and the door of the tiny bathroom. Shane sits on the bed eating his pie straight from the tin and chuckling at a DVD of *The Office* he's playing on the TV mounted on the wall. The pie is as good as always, the apples soft but not mushy, the tartness balancing the sweet and cinnamon flavors. The crust is perfectly flaky. Shane imagines Claire uses lard, although if she does, she probably doesn't advertise that fact. Shane's mom used to say you needed lard for truly flaky pie crusts. He wishes he could hear what his mom would have to say about Claire's pies.

Shane refocuses on the sitcom. It's not good to think about what he's lost this late at night. He won't sleep well. Better to marvel in Jim's pranks and Michael's cluelessness. The hilariously mundane problems of pre-pandemic life are comforting after a day like today.

There's a knock at the passenger window.

Slaughter, napping by the bed, is immediately alert and growling.

"Easy boy," Shane whispers. They're inside the loading area fence, and bandits seldom knock. But Shane gets his 9mm anyway.

Shane peeks carefully out the window. Does a double take. A middle-aged man in cargo pants and a poofy jacket stands there, his eyes darting from side to side above his N95 mask. He's got town written all over him. But if he's from Mt. Tucker, what's he doing outside the perimeter? And if he's not, how did he get into the loading yard?

Shane opens the door.

The man's eyes go to Shane's gun. He shifts uncomfortably. Then he takes a deep breath and sticks out his right hand. "My name's Joe Harding. I live in Mt. Tucker."

"Which is a clean zone," Shane replies. "You shouldn't be out here."

"Are you sick?"

"No."

"Then this is worth the risk."

Shane eyes him warily. "What is?"

"I need to hire you."

"Talk to Frank. I have a small load tomorrow. I'm sure he can accommodate you." Shane starts to close the door, but Joe grabs it.

"Not for shipping. See, my daughter, Dawn... she ran away earlier tonight. I want you to bring her back."

This smells like trouble. Shane doesn't need trouble. "I'm not in that business."

Joe shuffles his feet, looks around nervously. "Can I come in?"

Joe certainly seems harmless. Shane slips the gun into his waistband and settles back into the driver's seat.

Joe climbs onto the passenger seat and closes the door softly. He hunches low, leaning back from the light. He's breaking all kinds of rules being out beyond the perimeter. But Shane understands. People will do a lot for their children.

"See, my daughter's got this boyfriend," Joe says. "He lives in another clean zone. They knew each other when they were kids and have been communicating online. I tried to put a stop to it, but you know. Teenage girls. When Dawn vanished, I questioned her little brother. He admitted Dawn and this boy made plans to run away tonight and meet in Renton tomorrow. She took an old raft from the garage, so I bet she's going down the Cedar River. It passes a half mile from here."

"That's very interesting but, as I said, I'm not in the daughter retrieval business."

Joe looks on the verge of crying. "Please, Mr. Carpenter. There's nobody else I can ask. Nobody that will go into the plague zones."

"There are plenty of people. Call the police in Renton."

"You don't understand. If folks here find out Dawn left quarantine, they won't let her back in. I can stall for a couple days... say she's got a migraine or something. But I can't involve the authorities. Besides, with everything that's going on, you really think they'll look for her?"

"I see your point," Shane admits. "How old is she?"

"Eighteen."

"Eighteen? She's an adult. Maybe you should let her go."

"She's naïve. She's lived her whole life in this town. These kids don't know what they're getting into. They'll get sick, or killed, or worse. It's not like I'm asking a favor. I'll pay you. Twenty-five thousand, cash."

That gets Shane's attention. He could really use an extra twenty-five grand. Still...

"I'm just a truck driver, Joe."

"Please, Mr. Carpenter, she's my daughter. If you had kids, you'd understand. I'd do anything for her. I'd give up my own life if it would bring her back."

Shane's eyes immediately go to the picture clipped to his visor. Suffocating sadness wells in his chest. He did have a kid… once.

"Okay, enough." Shane takes a deep breath. This is a bad idea. He should kick Joe out, forget all about this late-night visit.

But instead, he says, "I'll do it. Tell me everything you know."

Sunrise.

Pink tinged clouds against a pale blue sky. Cool, still air. The scent of moist pine and a hint of wildflower sweetness. The kind of morning that makes you happy to be alive.

Shane does his morning inspection of the truck, sipping the rich, dark-roast coffee he had delivered to the loading dock from Claire's. It's so much better than what he makes in the back of his cab.

But time is slipping away, and he has a job to do.

He unhooks the truck from the charging station. He opens the door to the cab and whistles for Slaughter, who's snuffling at something near the fence. Slaughter abandons his investigation and scampers over, tongue lolling out, tail wagging. Shane gestures, and Slaughter jumps into the cab. Shane climbs up after him.

Once he's settled in the driver's seat, Shane pulls up Little Zeke's number on his phone and punches the call button.

"Hello?" Little Zeke's voice is raspy, like he just woke up.

"It's Shane. I'll have the rest of the money soon... maybe four days."

"See you then." Little Zeke hangs up.

Shane sticks the phone on the dashboard holder and shakes out his hands. He can't get ahead of himself. He's been working toward the day he can get justice for his family for a long time, and it's tempting to start anticipating. But one step at a time. The step he's on right now is fundraising.

Shane starts the truck and pulls up to the loading area gate. It creaks open, triggered remotely by the guards in the tower. Shane pulls out of the Mt. Tucker loading area onto the road.

A few minutes later, he comes across the remains of the last motorcycle and gangster from the day before. He pulls to the side of the road. Puts on his N95 mask and grabs his binoculars.

He gets out, waving his arms and shouting to scare half a dozen crows from the body. Last he heard, crows weren't one of the species that carried the virus, but you can't be too careful. The birds retreat to a nearby tree, eyeing him warily. Shane eyes them right back.

It's too soon for the corpse to have developed a stench, but the insects have found it.

Shane ignores the human remains, goes to the wreckage of the motorcycle. Digs in the saddlebags. Finds a trio of hand grenades. Those could come in handy. He slips them in his jacket pockets.

A steep, wooded slope rises to a high ridge above the road. Shane heads into the trees on foot. Pine needles crunch under his boots.

He crests the ridge and finds a clearing overlooking the winding highway as it stretches into the distance. He scans the road with binoculars.

A couple miles ahead he sees what he's looking for:

The Piranhaz.

He didn't think they'd give up easily after he killed several of their number. There are probably two dozen of them waiting to ambush him. Some stand behind a roadblock formed by several cars. The rest are ensconced on two ridges on either side of the road. They are mostly dozing or drinking. He sees the one with the rainbow mohawk, the one he shot, now swathed in bandages and reclining against a tree, fast asleep.

But then he sees the lookout, perched on a thick branch a dozen feet up in a pine tree at the peak of one of the ridges. That gangster's alert, watching the highway.

Shane lowers his binoculars and smiles.

Chapter 4

Bones passes time by cutting shapes out of his empty, paper coffee cup with his bowie knife. In the passenger seat next to him, Tyler snores softly, the muffled beat of whatever music he's listening to bleeding out of his headphones. If only Bones could nap like that. He's bored and he drank too much last night. But his nervous energy and the coffee sloshing in his bladder won't let him doze.

Mouse, perched in a tree above the roadblock, shouts down, "He's coming!"

Finally. Bones jumps out of the Audi E-Tron GT and positions himself behind it. The other Piranhaz also rouse themselves from their slumbers and inebriation. Rainbow bounces over to Bones, all joyful anticipation. She racks a round into her assault rifle with a sharp *CLACK*. She should be using a handgun with her bad arm, but she always goes for the biggest gun available whether it's practical or not.

The truck appears around a bend. It's well armored, but nothing unusual. Bones draws his Desert Eagle semi-automatic pistol from his hip holster.

"If he tries to drive through the roadblock, be ready to run to the side of the road," Bones warns.

"This isn't my first ambush," Rainbow says.

Bones bites back the temptation to remind her of the previous day's failure.

The truck draws closer… the driver must have seen the roadblock by now, but he keeps coming. The back of Bones' neck tingles. What's this guy up to? He could try to plow through the roadblock, but he'd never make it considering how narrow the road is. That would be a newbie move, and from what Rainbow's said, this guy is no newbie.

Suddenly, the truck veers off the highway onto a rutted, overgrown side road.

"Damn," Rainbow growls. "He turned off on Old Mill Road."

Bones shakes his head. "He's an idiot. Old Mill Road's blocked a mile and a half up. He's trapped."

Rainbow grins. "It'll be easy then."

Bones nods. Guess this trucker isn't so super after all.

Bones shouts to the assembled gangsters, "Saddle up, Piranhaz. Go get him."

The Piranhaz grab their weapons and run to their cars and motorcycles. Bones grabs Rainbow. "You come with me." He leads her into the woods at a fast jog.

They emerge from the trees into overgrown fields less than two minutes later. Old Mill Road passes by a hundred yards ahead. There's a locked gate of heavy metal I-beams where the road goes through a berm. Several steel drums sit in front.

Bones smiles. “Even a big rig isn’t getting through that.”

And as if on cue, not-so-super-trucker’s truck appears out of the trees, barreling up the road toward the gate.

But he doesn’t slow down. Is this guy crazy?

Then, motion draws Bones’ eye to a tube mounted above the armor on the truck’s front wheel. A cover on the end of the tube has just flipped up, revealing–

A rocket.

The rocket *ROARS* out of the tube–

KABOOM!

–it blows the hell out of the gate in a thunderous explosion. The steel drums fly through the air, spraying arcs of sand from their ruptured sides.

Bones and Rainbow gape as the truck punches through the wreckage, sending a twisted I-beam skittering into the brush.

Bones turns to Rainbow. “Rockets. You didn’t tell me he had rockets.”

She is too stunned to respond.

SHANE

Closes the plastic cover over the rocket launch switches. Rockets aren’t cheap. Replacing that one and the bulletproof glass in his driverside window is going to wipe out nearly half of what he earned on the Mt. Tucker delivery. He’s lucky Joe Harding offered him the extra gig… assuming nothing goes wrong. Which is never a safe assumption these days.

He checks his mirrors. A squad of Piranhaz cars bounce along the road behind him, gaining fast. He isn't out of the woods yet.

The truck crosses a small wooden bridge spanning a shallow stream. Not much, but it'll do. Shane hits the brakes. The truck slides to a stop in a cloud of dust and groaning metal.

Shane grabs one of the grenades he took from the wreckage of the motorcycle. He hops out of the truck, scrambles back down the bank of the stream. Wedges the grenade into the support beam on one side of the bridge. Pulls the pin.

Then scrambles back up to the truck.

BONES

Watches the truck pull away as – *BOOM* – the little bridge explodes in a million pieces.

The pursuing Piranhaz roar through the pulverized gate–

And *SCREECH* to a stop at the now impassible stream. One of the cars rear-ends another. Not bad but embarrassing.

The gang turns and heads back the way they came – it's a Keystone Kops exercise in chaos.

As they zoom back into the woods, Bones just shakes his head. "I'm starting to dislike this guy."

Shane makes it to the main highway. His trick worked – the Piranhaz are nowhere to be seen… for now.

It's only a couple miles to where the highway meets and turns parallel to the Cedar River. Shane scans the wide, flat waterway as he drives, looking for Dawn and her raft. If she travelled all night, she should have gotten well past this point, but you never know.

He's gone about six miles when he sees the power generation dam ahead. It's protected by some serious guard towers. No raft is getting by that. Dawn would have had to continue on foot from there.

Shane pulls over just past the dam and looks down into the valley below. The highway snakes down a few miles to the riverside town of Ashford. If Shane's going to find the girl, that's where she'll be.

Assuming she's still alive.

Ashford is not a clean zone – it was hit hard by the pandemic. As Shane drives through the outer town, he passes mostly abandoned and burned-out buildings. Graffiti. Trash. Decay. Death. Occasionally there's a complex that is still occupied. Those are invariably surrounded by high walls patrolled by gun-toting guards. The truck's windows are rolled up, the AC on, but the stench of rot still intrudes into the cab.

Finally, Shane reaches the downtown area. There are few abandoned buildings here, but razor wire fences and security bars hint that occupation doesn't mean things are safe. Half the streetlights show signs of having been cannibalized for their copper wiring.

If the girl followed the river on foot down from the dam, she would have reached town sometime in the early morning. So, Shane starts by cruising Riverside Drive.

The river district was an industrial area that gentrified a few decades ago. Now it's returning to its rougher roots. It still would have been dark when Dawn arrived, and scary as hell for someone from a place like Mt. Tucker. She probably would have gone somewhere familiar – a chain restaurant or coffee shop. McDonalds or Starbucks or Taco Bell. Somewhere she could safely wait for daylight to find transportation to wherever she's going.

It doesn't take long to hit all the chain joints within two blocks of the water. Only a handful are still in business. Unfortunately, Dawn is not at any of them, nor do any of the employees cop to having seen her. Shane's getting hungry, so he heads for the river district restaurant he prefers: The Good Eats Diner.

The Good Eats Diner is a classic truck stop kind of place next to a warehouse. Shane pulls into the parking lot and backs into a row of detached trailers. He puts on his N95 mask. Dwayne, the attendant, approaches as Shane gets out.

"I need to board my trailer here for a couple days," Shane says. After all, if he hasn't found the girl in two days, he never will.

"Sure," Dwayne replies. "Rate's twenty-five bucks a day."

Shane hands him fifty dollars cash and pockets the claim check.

Dwayne helps Shane detach the trailer, and Shane gives him another ten bucks as a tip. Shane pulls his cab up to a space in front of the diner. Refills Slaughter's water dish. Heads inside.

A little bell tinkles as Shane steps through the door. A dozen or so patrons eat breakfast and mind their own business. A big, hand painted sign on the wall says:

IF YOU SHOW SYMPTOMS,
YOU WILL BE ASKED TO LEAVE.

Taped on the bottom is a sheet of paper with additional rules scrawled in felt marker:

NO WEAPONS
NO FIGHTING

The smell of bacon frying sets Shane's stomach rumbling. He slides up to the counter.

The waitress, Kim, a woman who would look grandmotherly if it weren't for the long scar running from her left eye down into her facemask, pours him a cup of coffee. "Morning, Shane. The usual?"

"Yep."

"Where you coming in from?"

"Mt. Tucker."

"Any problems with the Piranhaz?"

"Some. I handled it."

"Things are getting bad out there. Pirates hit three boats on the river this week, and the State Police ain't done nothing. You heading downriver today?"

"Not sure."

Kim raises an eyebrow. "You're not sure where you're going?"

"I'm looking for someone. She been in here this morning?" He shows Kim the picture on his phone, the one Joe sent him of Dawn in a cheerleader outfit, her blonde curls billowing in the breeze.

Kim squints at it. "Girlfriend run out on you? Looks kinda young."

"Nothing like that. Her Dad asked me to find her."

Kim takes the phone and studies the image.

Shane notices the reflection of a wiry teenager in a chrome napkin dispenser. The kid is staring at Shane from a booth. As Shane turns toward him, he buries his face in a menu.

The kid is clearly trying to fly under the radar: baggy jeans, hoodie sweatshirt, black facemask, and a knit cap pulled low over close-cropped, black hair. Sometimes gangs use teenagers like this to scout potential targets. Could be trouble.

Kim slides the phone back to Shane. "She looks familiar, but she ain't been in here today."

Shane puts his phone away.

The bell over the door tinkles. The teenager has just made a fast exit.

Shane looks at Kim. "I'll be right back."

Shane exits the diner, sidles up behind a parked truck, watches as the kid crosses the street.

The kid pulls off his facemask and glances nervously back over his shoulder – it's not a boy after all. It's Dawn. She's cut off and dyed her hair. Must have taped down her boobs, too. Shane smiles. Clever girl.

Shane follows, staying out of sight.

Dawn makes her way the two blocks down to the river's edge. She crouches behind a big trash bin outside the fence of a ferry terminal. Shane takes up a position in an alley across the street and watches.

At the terminal dock, a 150' ferry is loading vehicles and passengers onto its garage deck. Above the garage deck is a passenger deck, and the bridge is perched on top of that. A walkway runs around the outside of the passenger deck. Four large-caliber machine guns are mounted at each corner. Armed sailors make sure everything goes smoothly.

When the sailors aren't looking, Dawn hops the fence. She darts among the vehicles waiting to board. Creeps up to the back of a stake truck. Slips in among the plastic barrels it's hauling.

Shane steps out of the alley, is about to cross the street when a convoy of cars rounds the corner.

He ducks back into the alley.

It's the Piranhaz.

Shane presses himself into the shadows as they pass – half a dozen cars, half a dozen motorcycles – all painted with the piranha symbol. He sees the woman with the rainbow mohawk in a black Audi E-Tron GT with a homemade iron grill guard and spiked hubcaps. The driver is a guy with a skull tattooed on his bald head.

The gang rounds the far corner.

Back at the dock, the sailors motion the stake truck onto the ferry. They don't spot Dawn.

Shane hauls ass back up the alley toward the diner, muttering curses.

He bursts through the door. The bell tinkles.

Oatmeal and juice are waiting for him. He takes a quick swig of juice and tosses a couple bills on the counter. “No time for breakfast today.”

Kim’s eyes are fixed on something over his shoulder. “Looks like you didn’t quite take care of your trouble after all.”

Shane follows her gaze to the parking lot. The Piranhaz are pulling in.

“What should I tell them?” Kim asks.

“Tell them whatever they want to know. Just try not to tell them very fast.” Shane circles the counter and ducks through the kitchen door.

Chapter 5

It appears luck has finally turned Rainbow's way. The first trucker hangout they check in Ashford, and there's the crimson tractor cab with the bear claw symbol on the door parked right out front. The trailer is no longer attached, meaning super trucker is most likely inside the diner getting a bite to eat, although Rainbow can't see any sign of him through the big picture windows.

Bones sticks his arm out of the window of the Audi and twirls his finger in the air. The Piranhaz circle their vehicles in the parking lot.

"Remember," Rainbow says, "you promised me the trucker was mine."

"Sure," Bones grunts. "As long as the money's where you say it is."

The gangsters get out of their vehicles and gather around Bones.

"Ken, Mouse, you're with me," Bones says. "Tyler, watch the cars. The rest of you go inside with Rainbow and see if you can find him."

Bones grabs a shotgun out of the Audi and leads Ken and Mouse toward the truck.

Rainbow enters the diner, followed by a dozen other Piranhaz.

A waitress with a scar running down one side of her face regards them across the counter, arms folded, eyes steely. “We don’t serve troublemakers.”

“We’re not here to cause trouble,” Rainbow replies. “We’re looking for someone.”

The waitress snorts. “Lot of that going around.”

“The guy who drives that truck out there, the one with the bear claw symbol. Know him?”

“Which bear claw symbol?”

“There’s only one.”

“Oh, him. Yeah, I know him.”

Is this bitch purposely trying to be annoying? Rainbow’s tempted to add a new scar to the waitress’s face to show her the consequences of messing with the Piranhaz. But as much fun as it is to torture people, it usually doesn’t result in acquiring the desired information, at least not quickly. So, Rainbow smiles and says as pleasantly as she can, “Has he been in here this morning?”

“Yep. He only had coffee. No time for breakfast, I guess. Seemed like he was in a hurry.”

“Did he say where he was going?”

“Nope.”

“How long ago did he leave?”

“Oh, I guess it would have to be about three minutes ago.”

Rainbow's cool evaporates. "Three minutes! Which direction did he go? And don't you dare tell me you didn't see or some shit like that."

The waitress jerks a thumb back over her shoulder. "He left through the kitchen."

Rainbow gives the waitress the evil eye – now she *really* wants to teach this bitch a lesson about messing with the Piranhaz, but she also doesn't want to let the trucker get away.

Rainbow readies her AR-5, ignoring the pain that stabs through her wounded shoulder. She rounds the counter, storms through the kitchen door, the other Piranhaz close behind.

The kitchen is small. One chef and a busboy cower appropriately at the invaders. Nowhere for the trucker to hide. But there's a back door.

Rainbow kicks it open. The gangsters pour out into a back alley that stinks of urine and rot. The garbage bin by the door is padlocked. No sign of the trucker.

But he can't have gone far. "Spread out!" Rainbow growls. "Find him."

BONES

Picked his team because he knows they can get the job done. Mouse is small and wiry and crafty. You never want to make a bet with him – he always cheats, never gets caught. Ken is of medium build but somehow still physically intimidating. It's in his posture, a sense of coiled, waiting violence. Dead eyes stare out through long, stringy hair that doesn't really hide his pockmarked complexion.

The truck with the bear claw symbol is parked at the very edge of the first row of spaces running along the front of the diner. Bones, Ken, and Mouse creep up on the driver's side, which is conveniently against the lot's outer fence, out of sight of any casual observers.

Bones hops up on the footboard, looks in the pock-marked window of the truck–

And jumps back as a mean-looking dog *barks* and *snarls* up a storm on the other side of the glass.

"Good doggie. I've got something for you." Bones cocks the shotgun and nods to Mouse. Mouse steps up with a lock pick and goes to work on the door.

SHANE

Watches the Piranhaz split up and head each direction down the alley. None bothers to look up. If they did, they'd see him on the roof, and then he'd be in trouble. He turns and jogs quietly across the flat tarpaper to the front of the diner.

His truck is just below. Three Piranhaz, including the one with all the bone tattoos, are huddled by the driver-side door trying to break in. Inside the cab, Slaughter barks and growls. That's good – it'll make it harder for the gangsters to hear Shane coming.

He climbs down onto an awning below the diner's neon sign. Leaps the short gap to the roof of his truck, landing gently on the balls of his feet. Slips down the passenger side, staying out of view of the Piranhaz on the other side. He pulls the tiny emergency key out of his key fob and unlocks the passenger door. Opens it quietly, letting Slaughter out.

BONES

Grins as Mouse gets the lock open with a loud *click*. Bones puts the shotgun to his shoulder. “Okay, open it.”

Mouse pulls the door open.

Bones sweeps the cab with the shotgun. “Where the hell is the dog?”

Then a *GROWL* to their left tells them.

Their heads swivel to see–

The trucker covering them with a 9mm in one hand while holding the dog back by the collar with the other. “Toss the gun in the truck,” he commands. The dog snarls and snaps, spittle flying.

Rage churns in Bones’ chest. “How many bullets you got in that thing? I have a dozen men just a shout away.”

The trucker shrugs. “So, shout. They can help Slaughter lick your brains off the asphalt.”

Bones takes a deep breath to calm himself. Tosses the shotgun into the cab. No choice. The trucker got the drop on them. “Now what?”

“Turn around. Put your hands on the fence.”

Bones complies. Ken and Mouse follow his lead.

SHANE

Exhales. He figured it was a coinflip whether the gangsters did what he said or tried to fight back. If they chose to fight, Shane and Slaughter could probably have taken out these three, but after that, who knows. He’s still not out of trouble.

"Slaughter, *kego*," he commands. Slaughter hops inside the cab through the open driver-side door. Shane follows, keeping his gun trained on the bad guys.

He starts the engine, pulls out.

The moment the truck starts moving, the three gangsters draw pistols – fire at the fleeing vehicle – but the armor can handle small arms fire. One bullet leaves a divot in the windshield. Something else Shane's going to have to replace when this is over.

Shane pulls backward in an arc, turns toward the gate, aiming to bypass the clump of Piranhaz vehicles.

And then the black Audi pulls back into his path.

Well, that's the reason he installed the battering ram. Shane aims the truck straight for the car.

The truck crushes the Audi – spins it into the other Piranhaz vehicles–

The truck flies through the gate just as the rainbow-mohawked gangster and her buddies make it back to the parking lot.

Shane turns the wheel, careens out onto the street – too fast – the truck's weight shifts ominously – his left tires hop the far curb – he takes out a trash can before getting the truck back onto the roadway.

The truck is back under control, but it won't take long for the gangsters to untangle their vehicles and come after him. Shane needs an escape route. He rounds the corner at the end of the block…

And pulls up to the kiosk at the gate to the ferry terminal. "Got any room?"

The attendant nods. "You just made it. They're about to close the gate."

BONES

Curses until he's out of breath. Rainbow was right – they need to make this trucker pay. Tyler, Ken, and Mouse push the ruined Audi out of the way of the other vehicles. The Piranhaz mount up. Bones and Rainbow hop into Mouse's red Mustang Mach-E that's been plastered with punk rock bumper stickers to cover the sun-damaged paint job.

"What about me?" Mouse asks.

"Ride with Ken," Bones growls.

Bones pulls out of the diner parking lot, races down the block, skids around the corner. The truck is nowhere to be seen, but there's a ferry terminal just ahead.

Bones careens into the ferry entrance, hits the breaks before he slams into the closed gate.

"Sorry," the attendant squeaks. "You just missed it."

Bones jumps out of the Mustang, runs to the gate. Slams his hands against it.

The ferry is pulling away from the dock. Super trucker stands at the railing of the ferry's garage deck. He smiles and waves at Bones.

Bones chest feels like it's about to explode. He turns on the attendant. "Where is that ferry going?"

"Renton," the attendant says.

Bones turns to his men. "Piranhaz, we're going to Renton."

Shane pulls on his N95 mask and strolls along the middle row of vehicles on the ferry's garage deck. Most of the drivers and pedestrian passengers are on their way up to the lounge on the deck above.

Shane spots the stake truck. Moves to it. Peers into the load of plastic barrels in the bed.

Dawn huddles in a small gap between barrels.

Shane grabs the back of her collar and hauls her out.

Dawn squeals. "Hey! Let me go!"

"Dawn Harding, my name's Shane Carpenter. Your father sent me to bring you home."

Dawn pulls out of his grip. Crosses her arms. "Tell him I don't want to go home."

"Trust me, you'll be better off. The plague zone is not a happy place for someone like you."

"You don't know me. You're just some guy my dad paid because he's too chicken-shit to leave the clean zone himself."

"I know you're young, I know you're being stupid, and I know your dad loves you."

"Well, smart guy, now you know I'm not going back!"

Dawn tries to bolt away – but Shane shoots out a hand and grabs her arm. He pins her up against the truck. She struggles, but he's twice her weight.

Dawn stops struggling. The corners of her eyes crinkle – she's smiling under her mask. "Now who's being stupid?"

She lets out an ear-splitting *SCREAM.*

Shane clamps a hand over her mouth – but not quick enough.

A sailor appears at the end of the row. Shouts, "What's going on down there?"

Shane tries to seem casual. "Nothing."

But it doesn't look like nothing. The sailor pulls out a walkie-talkie. "Seaman Riggs to all available. I have an urgent security situation on the garage deck. Need assistance. Over."

Shane glares at Dawn. "Great. See what you've done?"

In seconds there are half a dozen sailors with guns surrounding them. Shane releases Dawn. One of the sailors pats Shane down, finds his 9 mm.

A trim, fastidious man wearing a captain's cap strides up. "Good morning. I'm Captain Quick. What's this all about?"

"He's trying to kidnap me!" Dawn cries.

Shane holds up his hands. "I'm just taking her home."

Quick looks confused. "Her?"

Shane pulls Dawn's shirt up, revealing an elastic bandage wrapped around her breasts.

"Hey! Pervert!" Dawn yanks her shirt back down.

"Let's see your faces," Quick says.

Shane pulls off his mask. "She's a runaway. Her father sent me to bring her home."

"He's lying," Dawn protests, her mask around her chin. "My father died in the pandemic." Tears well up in her eyes. Her lip trembles. Suddenly, she looks heartbreakingly vulnerable. Clearly a natural actress.

"Her father lives in Mt. Tucker," Shane says. "I've got his number; you can call him."

"Please, Captain," Dawn begs, "I'm just trying to get to my aunt in Renton. This guy followed me onto the ferry – that's why I was hiding. That number's probably for his creepy partner. Who knows what they want to do to me. Please protect me!"

Quick and the sailors are looking at Shane like he just killed their first puppy. "Lock him in the storage locker," Quick orders.

Two of the sailors grab Shane's arms.

Panic wells in Shane's chest. "You can't do that!"

Quick eyes him, unimpressed. "My boat. I can do anything I want." Then to Dawn, "Young lady, perhaps you'd be safer up in the lounge with the other passengers."

The two sailors drag Shane backwards toward a doorway. Dawn shoots him a smug smile.

"She's a stowaway!" Shane shouts.

Dawn's smugness evaporates.

Quick turns back to Shane. "What?"

The two sailors dragging Shane pause. "Check her ticket," Shane says.

Dawn adopts a sheepish expression. "I lost it."

Quick isn't buying that one. "Uh-huh. In that case, I think it would be better if you stayed up on the bridge with me. We'll let the authorities in Renton straighten all this out."

Now Dawn goes into flirt mode – fluttering eyelashes, hand on Quick's arm. "Don't you trust me, Captain? I'd be happy to sit with you, but we don't need to bother the police."

"That had a better chance of working when I thought you were male," Quick replies.

Now it's Shane's turn to shoot a smug look at Dawn.

Although it loses some of its impact as the two sailors push him through the door to the lower crew deck.

The sailors drag Shane down a staircase and shove him into a storage locker. They *slam* the heavy steel door. The latch mechanism *clanks* into place. Then, there's a soft, metallic *click* from the other side – a padlock no doubt.

Shane straightens his flannel shirt. The room is about six feet square, filled with supplies – cans of grease, coils of rope, spare parts, etc. A single, tiny porthole looks out over the river. Once the echoing steps of his captors recede, Shane tests the door. No surprise, it won't budge.

He sits on a crate and fumes.

Chapter 6

Captain Quick drags Dawn onto the bridge, his iron grip painful on her wrist. The first mate, a middle-aged guy with an ill-fitting uniform stretched over an ample gut, mans the wheel. He gives Dawn a disinterested glance, then returns his attention to his task. The bridge juts up above the upper deck, spanning the width of the ferry, wide windows offering a gorgeous view of the river, a silver-blue ribbon twinkling under partly cloudy skies.

Quick shoves Dawn into a swivel chair by the navigation table. “Stay there. If you try to run away, I’ll lock you up with your buddy.”

“He’s not my buddy,” Dawn grumbles. “What’s going to happen when we get to Renton?”

“We’ll turn you over to the police.”

A weight fills Dawn’s belly. What if they throw her in jail? What will happen to her then? “Please, I wasn’t trying to cause trouble. It’s just, I don’t have any money, and I have to get to Renton.”

Quick snorts. “We get punks like you every other trip. You think because of the pandemic all the rules are off. Well, this ferry is still a business. The only way my crew and I eat is if it stays in business. You stow away, you're doing more than stealing from us. You're jeopardizing our living."

"I'm really, really, really sorry. I'll pay you back, I promise. Just let me go to Renton. Please?"

Quick looks at her skeptically. "What's so important in Renton? And don't say your aunt."

Maybe it's time for the truth. Maybe this Captain Quick is a romantic. "My boyfriend."

Quick rolls his eyes. "You're a cute girl. You don't need to go to all this trouble to get laid."

"I love him!" Dawn protests.

"Love, huh?"

"Yeah. Something a cold-hearted prick like you wouldn't know anything about."

Quick turns on her, suddenly savage. "Don't tell me what I know!"

"I'm sorry." A tear tickles Dawn's cheek. She wipes it away, trying to make it look like she's rubbing something out of her eye, but her hand trembles. She probably isn't fooling anyone.

Quick's expression softens just a bit. "So, you love this boy?"

"Yes."

"And he loves you?"

"Yes."

"You're sure?"

Maybe this Quick is a romantic after all. "Of course. We're going to get married."

Quick snorts. “Married doesn’t equal love. But if this guy loves you as much as you say, I’m sure he’ll bail you out.”

Dawn clenches her fists. “You’re a bastard.”

The first mate interrupts this repartee. “Captain! We’ve got unwelcome company.”

“Where?”

“Coming up on our aft.”

Quick grabs a pair of binoculars and peers out one of the smaller windows to the rear of the bridge.

Dawn creeps up beside him. Half a dozen Jet Skis zoom toward the ferry. Painted black. Skull and crossbones on the sides. Rooster tales of spray trailing behind.

Quick growls, “Sound the alarm.”

The first mate hits a button, and a deafening *CLANG-CLANG-CLANG* shakes the ferry.

On the deck below, sailors run to the fixed machine guns at the aft of the ferry.

The Jet Skis, ridden by scruffy rednecks, spread out across the river about a quarter mile back.

One of the sailors opens fire with the big gun – the thunderous *RAT-A-TAT-TAT* punctuated by the *CLATTER* of .50 caliber shells hitting the deck.

The Jet Skis bob and weave as bullets churn up the river. The small craft are fast and unpredictable – difficult to hit with the bulky machine gun.

But not impossible.

Gunfire sweeps across one of the pirates – shredding him and his Jet Ski.

But the rest get in next to the ferry – too close for the mounted guns to target. They toss smoke bombs up onto the decks near the front of the vessel.

As the ferry chugs forward, the dark grey smoke drifts back, obscuring Dawn's view of what's happening below.

The *roar* of multiple gas engines draws Dawn's gaze upriver. The second wave of pirates approaches. They ride in three battered speedboats, half a dozen in each. Armed to the teeth. Trailing the speedboats is a small, flat barge.

The speedboats zoom into the smoke cloud surrounding the ferry.

A chill washes over Dawn.

Shane presses his face to the supply closet's porthole, trying to see what's caused the alarm. Smoke is coming from somewhere. A fire? Hopefully they don't forget he's locked up down here.

A grappling line goes up right past him. He ducks out of sight as pirates clamber up the rope in leather vests and fishing boots, kerchiefs up around their mouths and noses like Old West bandits, goggles protecting their eyes from the stinging smoke.

So that's what caused the alarm.

Shane looks around for a weapon. Finds a tool chest and pops it open. There's a screwdriver… that might work. Then he notices the crowbar in the corner.

He grabs the crowbar and positions himself beside the door.

He waits to see what's going to come through it.

Enough smoke seeps into the bridge to tickle Dawn's nose even through her N95 mask. Gunfire and screams echo up through the haze, but she can't see more than a few feet past the windows. She might as well sit back down, stay away from the glass in case of stray bullets.

Sweat beads on the first mate's forehead. "What are they doing? River pirates have never hit a boat this big, this well armed."

Quick strides across the bridge. "It looks like they've been recruiting. I've never seen this many together before." He retrieves a pistol from a drawer. "Stop the engine before we hit something. Drift with the current. Try to keep us in the middle of the river."

"Captain, shouldn't you stay on the bridge?" the first mate asks.

"My crew and my passengers are dying down there. I'm going to do something about it."

"What about me?" Dawn asks.

"You stay here." And Quick goes out the door to join the fight.

Heavy footsteps approach the storage room door. Sounds like two people. Shane chokes up on the crowbar and lifts it above his shoulder, the way he was taught to hold a bat in Little League.

KA-BANG!

KA-BANG!

Someone's beating on the padlock.

CRACK-CLANG.

A pause. Then, the door's locking mechanism slides up.

A scraggly pirate in a tobacco-stained tank top bursts through the door, a fire axe dangling from his hand. Sloppy. Must not have been expecting anyone to be inside.

Shane takes a home run swing to the pirate's face. *CRACK*!

That guy goes down.

Shane leaps out into the hallway–

Another pirate – big belly, long beard – raises a shotgun–

Shane swings – *CRUNCH* – the crowbar connects with the pirate's jaw. Blood sprays across the wall. Pirate number two joins his buddy in a heap on the floor.

Shane drops the crowbar, retrieves the shotgun and the first pirate's .45 revolver. Jogs up the passage.

Dawn shifts nervously in the chair by the navigation table. Muffled gunfire and indistinct shouts continue to echo up from below. The first mate grips the wheel, his knuckles white, sweat dripping down his temples.

A bloodcurdling scream – somewhere close. The first mate spins, eyes wide and darting, searching for the source.

Enough of this. Dawn's not going to sit here waiting to die.

She bolts for the door.

"Hey, come back!" the first mate shouts. But she's gone before he can do anything to stop her.

Dawn runs down the stairs to the smoke-filled passenger lounge. Her eyes water, her throat burns. She stifles a cough. Sound is muffled and distant in the haze.

She crouches behind a row of padded chairs. She needs to find somewhere safe, and nowhere on the ferry seems likely to be safe. That means she needs to figure out a way to get to shore. There are lifeboats outside, but she has no idea how to launch one. Could she even do it alone? Swimming is her best bet. If she can get down to the garage deck and to a railing, it wouldn't be far to dive into the river.

BANG – Something slams against the window behind her – she spins toward it.

On the walkway outside, a pirate with a gas mask has a sailor pushed up against the window. They're wrestling over a shotgun. The pirate elbows the sailor in the face – a sickening *CRACK* – the sailor falls to his knees. The pirate rips the shotgun away – turns it on the sailor—

Dawn scrambles away. Don't look back… don't look… *BLAM.*

Dawn doesn't look back.

But she pulls up short at the end of the row of chairs. A body is sprawled in the aisle – a young man, a passenger, blood pooled in a vicious exit wound on his back.

Dawn maneuvers gingerly over the body, trying to stay low, out of sight of anyone outside the windows. She scrambles down the next row of seating, reaches the other side of the ferry. There's a stairway down to the garage deck five feet away.

She creeps down the stairs, blinking away tears from the smoke. Well, mostly from the smoke.

Reaches the garage deck, dives in between the closest cars.

She moves to the aisle between the rows of vehicles, makes her way forward in a crouch, heart thudding in her chest.

A cackle of laughter – she ducks between two cars.

Peeks into the next aisle. Two pirates are tormenting a middle-aged couple huddled together on the deck. The pirates feint at their victims with knives, laughing at the couple's panic.

BLAM – one of the pirates is blown back against a pickup truck. He slides to the ground, leaving a chunky smear of red on the pickup's passenger door.

The other pirate spins – the gunman is Captain Quick – coming up the aisle–

Quick fires again, takes down the second pirate. The couple gape at Quick – their guardian angel. "Get forward," he barks.

The couple scramble to their feet. Dash away. Quick turns–

And a pirate appears from behind a van – jams a hunting knife into Quick's gut.

Quick stares at the pirate in shock. The pirate slaps the pistol from Quick's hand. Withdraws the knife with a hard slash. Quick slumps to the deck, blood spilling from his belly.

That's more than enough for Dawn. She scrambles back – through a door–

And right into a barrel-chested pirate.

Dawn cries out – tries to run–

The pirate grabs her around the neck with one beefy hand – slams her back against the wall. Pain ricochets through her skull – stars twinkle in her vision.

The pirate tips back his greasy baseball cap with his free hand. Even through the gaiter pulled up over his nose, his breath stinks of coffee and chaw and poor hygiene. He looks Dawn up and down. "Well, ain't you fine. Bet you'll be worth a bundle."

And he slings her over his shoulder.

Chapter 7

Shane readies the shotgun. Eases open the door to the starboard outer walkway on the passenger deck.

The smoke is thick outside. A dozen feet away, a pirate in a leather vest, red ballcap and matching red bandana hunches over the body of a dead sailor, searching his pockets.

Shane inches out onto the deck….

The door *creaks–*

The pirate spins, goes for his gun–

Shane fires – blows the pirate back over the railing.

Shane steps to the railing, watches the body splash into the river.

Ten yards forward along the walkway, one of the smoke bombs sputters, fizzles out.

The air clears as the ferry gradually drifts out of the cloud of smoke. Shane scans the river.

Near the aft of the ferry, the pirates' barge is pulling away. It's about twenty-five feet long with a pilot console at the front. One pirate drives while two others, armed with assault rifles, watch over a huddle of young, female prisoners.

Dawn sits on the edge of that cluster, knees pulled up to her chest, hands bound in front of her.

Shane runs down the walkway toward the rear of the ferry. Finds a Jet Ski bobbing beside the ferry, tethered with a grappling hook. Just what he needs. He climbs over the railing and shimmies down the rope to the Jet Ski.

He releases the grappling line, hits the ignition. The engine *roars* to life. Shane squeezes the accelerator and zooms off after the barge, icy spray and chill wind tearing at his clothes and hair.

Shane's commandeered Jet Ski closes fast on the slower barge. The pirate guards turn toward the whining *growl* of the Jet Ski's engine. When they see Shane, they raise their assault rifles–

Shane levels the shotgun at the guard in the rear of the barge, farthest from the prisoners. He doesn't want to risk injuring any innocents with the pellet spray.

BOOM!

Turns out the shotgun is loaded with slugs. Shane hits the guard dead center of his chest. The guard tumbles into the river.

The prisoners scream and hunch down on the deck of the barge. The second guard opens fire with his assault rifle–

TAT-TAT-TAT-TAT!

A handful of bullets cut a line down the front of Shane's Jet Ski – but he's still going. He bobs, weaves, zigs, zags – dodging a hail of metal.

DAWN

Surveys the situation. She doesn’t want to go with this brute that her dad hired to take her home, but it’s far better than whatever these river pirates have in store for her. Only, the brute is a bit outgunned. If she wants to escape, she’d better do something to help him.

She springs up, lunges at the remaining guard, grabs at the assault rifle with her bound hands. They wrestle for control of the weapon. He’s bigger, stronger, and his wrists aren’t tied together. But while they struggle, he can’t shoot at…

SHANE

Can’t believe what he’s seeing. This girl’s got balls. It could get her killed.

No longer under fire, he quickly pulls up to the barge. Leaps onboard. The pirate at the wheel draws a pistol–

Shane blows him away with a shotgun blast.

Shane turns toward the back of the boat – just in time to see Dawn and the pirate guard tumble overboard, still wrestling for the assault rifle. Shane runs back. He can’t see either of them in the murky water.

DAWN

Struggles with the pirate, drifting slowly down into the darkness. The water is cold, cold enough that the shock of it stuns her. The pirate manages to rip the gun out of her hand. He kicks for the surface.

SHANE

Sees the pirate's head burst up out of the water, the man gasping for breath through his soaked bandana. Dawn surfaces a couple yards away. The pirate brings the gun up toward her – she desperately kicks back–

And Shane puts a shotgun slug into the pirate's temple. The contents of the pirate's head blow out of the opposite temple, forming a disgusting slick on the surface. The pirate sinks out of sight.

Shane extends a hand for the girl, but Dawn swims for the Jet Ski that he abandoned, bobbing nearby. Dang it, doesn't this girl have any sense at all? He's trying to save her life.

Shane scrambles through the screaming prisoners to the wheel of the barge, turns it back toward Dawn. She climbs onto the Jet Ski, rips off her drenched facemask and hits the ignition. She aims the Jet Ski downriver.

The sound of more engines joins theirs. Shane looks back.

Other pirates have spotted them. Two speedboats zoom from the ferry. Each one carries three pirates.

The speedboats split up – one goes after Dawn, the other after the barge.

Dawn guns the Jet Ski to full speed. Shane guns the barge – but it can't go nearly as fast. The second speedboat closes in.

One of the pirates fires a burst from an AK-47 into the air over the barge. The prisoners scream and duck. "Throw out your weapons!" the pirate commands.

Shane looks at the prisoners. They're terrified.

The pirate fires another burst into the air.

Shane can't let the pirates capture them. They'd kill him immediately, and the fate of the prisoners would be nearly as bad. He looks around frantically for a way out.

And spots a box of smoke bombs under the console.

He grabs one, pulls the pin. Drops it onto the deck of the barge as smoke billows out of the squat canister.

In moments the barge is engulfed in a dark cloud. Shane holds his breath. Hopefully the pirates won't want to fire blindly into the smoke for fear of hitting some of their human booty.

THUD – the speedboat pulls alongside the barge.

Shane crouches down with the prisoners. Two shadowy figures come through the haze.

Shane fires the shotgun at one – *BLAM.*

The pirate falls back, and Shane is on the move, scrambling through the smoke.

He reaches the edge of the barge where the speedboat is tied. Levels the shotgun at the pirate behind the wheel, pulls the trigger–

Click.

The pirate at the wheel draws his pistol, *fires* as Shane leaps. The bullet *sizzles* by Shane's ear. Shane wallops the driver with the shotgun, sending him tumbling back.

Shane drops the empty shotgun, draws the .45 revolver–

The pirate rolls over, raises his gun for a second shot – *BLAM* – too late. Shane puts a bullet between his eyes.

TAT-TAT-TAT – a burst of gunfire from the barge – followed by *screams* – Shane spins, ducks.

The pirate on the barge has found the smoke grenade, tosses it into the river. As the smoke clears, he unleashes a second volley into the air. The prisoners cower and cry.

"Everybody down on the deck!" the pirate commands. "Where is he?!"

One prisoner points toward the speedboat with a trembling finger.

The pirate spins toward Shane–

But Shane has the drop on him.

"Throw down your gun," Shane growls.

The pirate goes pale. Complies.

Shane motions with the pistol. "Into the water."

The pirate jumps into the river. One of the prisoners, a woman in her twenties, scrambles to take the wheel of the barge.

Shane gives her a nod. "Good luck."

Then he grabs the wheel of the speedboat and hits the throttle. The boat spins away from the barge. Shane aims upriver after Dawn and her pursuer as the prisoners guide the barge toward shore.

DAWN

Pushes the Jet Ski as fast as she can, but it's not fast enough. The pirates' speedboat is gaining.

Dawn releases the throttle, dives the Jet Ski nose into the water, spinning it in a 180. Almost throws herself off into the river. Prior to today, she's driven a personal watercraft exactly once, on a trip to Mirror

Lake when she was eleven, back before they sealed off Mt. Tucker from the pandemic.

She squeezes the throttle, zooms back upriver – right past the speedboat as it slows to turn after her in a tight arc. She's bought herself a minute or two, but the pirates are gaining again. The wind whips at her wet clothes, numbing her skin.

Another speedboat races toward her from upriver and her throat tightens in panic – until she sees that the boat's piloted by that brute her dad hired, Shane. She's got to hand it to him; the guy is determined.

She veers, passes by him only a few feet away. If he can keep the pirates occupied, maybe she can get to safety. But whatever happens, she's not letting him take her back home.

SHANE

Is hit by spray from Dawn's Jet Ski as she flies by on his port side.

He aims the speedboat right at the pirates pursuing her, forcing them to veer to his right. They rake the starboard side of his boat with gunfire as he passes. None of the bullets hit him, though.

Shane makes a hard U-turn, chases the pirates who are chasing Dawn.

He pulls parallel to the pirates – exchanges wild shots with them. This is crazy. He has no idea how many bullets are even in his scavenged pistol. Why is he risking his life for this girl?

DAWN

Pulls away from the two speedboats. Shane's doing exactly what she hoped, keeping the pirates busy. Sneaking onto the ferry was a disaster, no question, but if she can get to shore, maybe she can get back on track.

Then she spots two more pirates on Jet Skis approaching from upriver. Those guys are pretty determined, too. She scans the river, planning how she can get by them…

And then her Jet Ski engine sputters.

She looks at the fuel gauge.

Empty.

Shit.

The Jet Ski skips to a stop. Bobs in the middle of the river. Dawn looks over her shoulder. Behind her – Shane and the pirates in speedboats. Ahead – pirates on Jet Skis. All are closing fast.

SHANE

Squints into the biting wind. Dawn is dead in the water. Everyone's closing in on her. Shane's outnumbered and outgunned. He needs to be clever if he's going to get both Dawn and him out of this alive.

He grabs a grappling hook coiled nearby.

The pirates' speedboat bears down on Dawn. Shane veers sideways – *slams* into the pirates – fiberglass and wood crack–

He knocks them off course. The two boats fly past Dawn, Shane between her and the pirates.

Shane tosses the grappling hook – it catches inside the pirates' speedboat–

The pirates open fire on Shane yet again – bullets perforate the hull around him, shatter the low windshield – one rips through his flannel sleeve, missing him by a hair.

Shane veers away – the grappling line goes taut between the two speedboats–

Which is bad news for the pirates on Jet Skis. They suddenly find themselves flying toward a line stretched between two boats.

WHAM – the Jet Skis hit the line – the pirates tumble through the air, splash into the river.

Two down.

One of the pirates on the speedboat cuts the grappling line. The boats are untethered again.

The pirates' speedboat arcs around, comes back for Shane. He dives under the dash as they shred his boat with gunfire.

A bullet hits his outboard – cuts the fuel line–

KABOOM – the engine explodes – taking off the back third of his boat.

But as the pirates go by, they cross the grappling rope trailing in the water from a cleat on the side of Shane's boat. The line tangles in the pirate's propeller. Their engine grinds to a stop.

Shane has no interest in being tied to these guys anymore. He quickly frees the line on his end. But his boat is in bad shape. The mangled stern is quickly disappearing below the surface of the river.

The two crippled boats float downriver with the current. One pirate jumps in the water to untangle their prop as their boat drifts ahead of Shane.

Meanwhile…

DAWN

Jumps off her useless Jet Ski back into the frigid river. She swims to one of the Jet Skis that was knocked over by the grappling line.

With a heave, she rights it. Climbs on. Hits the ignition – *VROOM* – it works!

SHANE

Tries to bail water out of his speedboat with his cupped hands. It's pointless – this boat is obviously going down no matter what he does – but it's all he can think to do.

Dawn circles around the disabled pirate boat on her Jet Ski, giving them a wide berth. They ignore her for the moment, more occupied with trying to untangle their prop.

She motors up a dozen yards away from Shane. "Thanks for saving me."

"Come get me!" Shane shouts.

"Why should I? You'll just take me home."

Shane's neck grows warm with embarrassment. "I can't swim."

"Good. Then you can't follow me." And she pulls away, heading downriver.

Shane pounds the dash of the speedboat with his fist. Bitch. Fine, see how you fare on your own.

DAWN

Should feel relieved, but guilt gnaws at her. She looks back. Shane's going down fast. She bites her lip.

He did save her life… it really wouldn't be right to leave him to drown.

Something floats by in the river. A body. Wearing a foam life vest.

Dawn guides the Jet Ski up next to it. Unhooks the vest. It has a bullet hole in it but seems functional.

She swings back around, motors close to the sinking speedboat, tosses the life vest to Shane. "Here."

He catches it. "Thanks."

But as she peels away – the sound of an engine starting. The pirates in the other speedboat have untangled their prop.

Dawn makes a dash for shore. The pirates take off in pursuit.

Chapter 8

Shane watches helplessly as Dawn beaches the Jet Ski and scrambles into the trees.

The pirates' speedboat reaches shore. The three pirates jump out and charge after her.

Shane pulls on the life vest and tightens the straps. The water creeps up the sloped deck of what remains of his speedboat, only a few feet from his toes now.

Now what does he do? The ferry is drifting up behind him. Shore seems miles away, although it's probably no more than a hundred yards. The ferry is closer and getting even closer by the second.

Shane takes a deep breath and jumps into the river.

The cold punches into his bones. His head goes under, and panic floods through him. His chest heaves, his arm flail, reaching for anything and finding nothing.

But the life vest works. He pops back to the surface. He gasps in deep breaths, trying to calm his racing heart.

He dogpaddles toward the ferry, fighting the terror that hovers at the edge of his vision. Why didn't he ever learn to swim?

He paddles around to the side of the ferry so it won't crush him. The boat is eerily quiet, the combat over, the engines off. As it looms close, the size of the vessel overwhelms him. The deck is at least fifteen feet above the water line. How is he going to get back onboard?

He spots a grappling line trailing into the water. That's his chance. He kicks up next to the massive boat.

He lunges up out of the water as the rope goes by, catches the line with his right hand. The ferry drags him, but it's floating with the current, so the force is minimal. Shane gets his other hand on the rope and pulls himself up out of the water.

He climbs up the rope, hand over hand, his arms burning. Reaches the railing. Flops over, onto the deck. He sucks in big breaths as chilly river water pools around him, mixing with the blood and grime on the rough, textured steel. There are a couple bodies visible. No sign of any living people.

And no time to rest. Shane pulls himself to his feet, his legs and arms and shoulders aching from his panicked dogpaddle and rope climb. He ditches the life vest. He has no intention of going back in that river.

He finds the stairs to the upper deck. Lunges up, three steps at a time. Bursts onto the bridge.

Empty. The ferry is drifting freely.

If he's going to retrieve Dawn, he needs to get off this boat ASAP, ideally with his truck.

He grabs a pair of binoculars, looks upriver. In the distance ahead, the river bends to the right. A long, wooden fishing dock extends toward the ferry from shore.

Shane sets the throttle on low to keep the ferry from drifting. He aims for the dock and locks the wheel.

Shane runs down to the auto deck, sprints to the forward loading gate. Throws the locking handle. Slides it open.

The ferry is closing on the fishing dock. Right on target. The dock is about six feet lower than the ferry's garage deck, but that's the least of Shane's problems. There's no time to get back to the bridge to stop the ferry.

Shane dashes to his truck. There are two cars between it and the loading gate. He climbs in, starts the engine. Pulls forward.

The truck's battering ram hits the car directly in front. Shane eases the accelerator down – pushing the car. It strikes the next car – now he's pushing both. The first car slides through the loading gate – tumbles into the river. The second car follows.

Shane throws the truck in reverse. Backs up as far as he can. He has a clear shot for the gate. Shifts back into drive.

The ferry slowly approaches the dock – head on.

When it's a few yards away, Shane hits the accelerator.

He shoves the pedal to the floor, pushing the truck to speed up as fast as possible – which is not very fast in a vehicle this heavy.

The ferry crashes into the dock with a sharp *CRACK* – planks fly into the air–

Shane launches the truck off the ferry–

It drops six feet – *CRUNCHES* onto the dock – swerves, tires squealing against wet wood – Shane fights the wheel, regains control, straightens the truck on the dock.

But the ferry hasn't slowed one bit. It chews through the dock mere feet behind Shane's truck, tossing planks through the air. The *RUMBLE* is relentless, punctuated by the *SNAP* of oiled lumber.

Shane accelerates, trying to outrun the ferry–

BOOM – the ferry hits ground – lurches to a stop–

The wave of water thrown forward by the massive boat swamps the dock – it slews sideways–

And Shane makes shore just as the remains of the dock collapse into the river behind him.

Shane pulls the truck to a stop. Looks back at the grounded ferry. His heart pounds with a ferociousness that makes him lightheaded.

But there's no time to catch his breath now. He roars off down the road.

Dawn scrambles through the trees, wet needles crunching softly underfoot, the pirates in pursuit, whooping and taunting somewhere behind her. It's easy to stay ahead of them – thank you soccer – but she can't seem to shake them either.

She emerges from the woods at the edge of an abandoned amusement park. It was a small-town type of place, and it's in bad shape. Ferris wheel tumbled over. Boardwalk games ransacked and collapsing. Tilt-a-Whirl tilted but not whirling.

Dawn dashes into the park.

The pirates emerge from the woods behind her. One shouts, "Where you going, girlie?"

Dawn wishes she knew. Maybe she can lose them in the ruins of the amusement park or find somewhere to hide and wait until they get bored searching for her. She sprints for the closest enclosed structure – the haunted house ride, a low, wide building with cartoony ghosts and monsters illustrated on the side in fading paint. Dark and brooding, it probably looks scarier now than when kids queued up between the aluminum handrails.

Dawn vaults those handrails, runs past the ticket kiosk, through the entry arch, past two-seater carts lined up on the rails. Rats scatter as she claws through dangling strips of thin, black cloth that tickle her face. The place is a shambles. Real cobwebs outnumber the fake ones. The air is dank and still. Dawn climbs over a dusty ride car, ducks under rubber bats, nearly turns her ankle stepping on an old beer can.

She moves into the guts of the ride. It's dark. Really dark. She reaches out to keep from bumping into things – her fingertips brushing against wooden walls with flaking paint and damp, soft props that cause her to recoil instinctively.

But she hears the pirates enter the building behind her. She keeps pushing forward.

The graveyard room. Her eyes are starting to adjust. She sees tombstones, skeletons, ghosts made of thin cloth hanging limply from their fishing line. She can make out a coffin. She opens it – and screams as a glowing corpse springs out.

Fake of course.

She punches its head off, angry she fell for that.

The pirates are cackling somewhere nearby. Dawn climbs into the coffin, pulls the lid closed.

She's wedged in with what's left of the fake corpse. Holds her breath as she hears the pirates enter the room.

One says, "Where the hell did she go?"

There's a *thump*. Another voice: "Ow! I can't see shit in here!"

Dawn covers her mouth to stifle her giggle.

The pirates' footsteps fade away. Dawn climbs out of the musty coffin and creeps back toward the entrance. She starts to breathe easier as she moves through those strips of black cloth, the loading area just ahead, daylight spilling in from the entry arch–

And then the pirates emerge from the exit tunnel opposite her.

They blink at her in surprise.

Then they grin.

They're closer to the archway than she is.

Shit. Dawn darts back into the ride, the pirates hot on her tail.

She passes through the graveyard room, doesn't stop. Reaches a cheesy Egyptian mummy room. A square outlined in sunlight reveals a maintenance door. Escape!

Dawn dives through the door–

Into the dazzling sunlight, down a couple steps.

She finds herself in a field of mounded garbage, clouds of flies buzzing across it in waves. The stench of rot turns her stomach. Apparently, someone is using this as a dump.

And in the middle of this field of debris is an adorable little girl of about four. Her long blond hair hangs in limp, dirty strands, a filthy nightgown her only protection from the elements. A threadbare teddy bear dangles from her hand. She looks at Dawn with heart-meltingly big eyes.

Dawn's stomach turns again. What will the pirates do with a cherubic child like this?

Dawn yells, "Run, little girl! Run!"

But Teddy Bear Girl just stares blankly at her.

And then the pirates burst out of the haunted house.

Dawn dashes for Teddy Bear Girl – the pirates pursue – only steps behind–

One pirate gets within arm's length – lunges for Dawn–

And then the ground drops out from under her.

Dawn pitches forward – reaches out – catches the far edge of the pit with the fingertips of both hands – slams into the side, knocking the air out of her. The pirate isn't so lucky – he skids on loose trash – plunges into the pit.

Pit?

Dawn looks down. It's a tiger trap – someone dug an eight-foot-deep hole, covered it with cardboard and trash.

The other two pirates slide to a stop at the edge of the pit–

And suddenly a dozen scavenger kids burst from hiding places scattered in the debris. These kids aren't cute like Teddy Bear Girl – they look almost feral. They range in age from about six to twelve – filthy, ragged clothes, wild tangles of hair, makeshift weapons.

Several of the kids charge the two pirates at the edge of the pit – shove them from behind–

The shocked pirates tumble on top of their buddy – the kids dive in after. Dawn turns away from the pirates' *screams* and the sounds of *rending flesh*–

And finds Teddy Bear Girl looking down at her, *snarling*.

Teddy Bear Girl stomps on Dawn's right hand. Pain shoots through Dawn's fingers.

"Hey!" Dawn grabs Teddy Bear Girl's foot, twists. Teddy Bear Girl falls back.

Dawn pulls herself up out of the pit, toes slipping against the dirt wall, hands threating to lose their grip on the loose garbage. But she makes it.

She glances back down – and almost loses her lunch.

But she has more pressing needs than what the scavenger kids are doing to those poor pirates. Teddy Bear Girl is up and charging her again. Dawn shoves the four-year-old away easily.

But several other kids are scrambling toward them now. Dawn takes off, dashing across the debris. She should be able to outrun these kids and their short legs, but she keeps slipping in the damn mushy piles of trash – and the kids are strangely sure-footed.

They herd her toward a row of sideshow attractions. At least the ground there is solid.

Dawn sprints down the dirt path, finally putting distance between her and the kids. And then she realizes why they herded her that way.

Dead end.

The path once led into a food court, but the entrance is now boarded up with plywood painted with a mural of unicorns and leprechauns.

She spins around. The kids – all of them – stalk toward her. The ones who jumped in the pit have blood smeared around their mouths like watermelon juice. There's death in their eyes.

Dawn presses back against the plywood wall. She scans the sideshow attractions desperately for a way out.

BANG – a gunshot!

From behind the kids. It's Shane, standing on a pile of rubble. He holds his pistol pointed into the air. "Stay away from her!"

The kids stare at him.

Unimpressed.

They turn in unison and continue their march toward Dawn.

Teddy Bear Girl giggles and scrambles ahead of the others. Shane yells, "Stop!" but Teddy Bear Girl ignores him.

Shane aims–

BLAM – puts a bullet through Teddy Bear Girl's teddy bear.

Teddy Bear Girl looks down in shock. Bits of stuffing drift from the hole in the bear's abdomen.

Teddy Bear Girl's lower lip begins to quiver. And then she *WAILS*, crying like...

...well, like a four-year-old whose teddy bear just got shot.

The scavenger kids back away, fixing Shane with murderous looks.

Dawn steps forward, cautiously.

The kids hold their positions.

Dawn makes her way through them, trying to move slowly but not too slowly. They glare at her with murderous fury.

She reaches Shane. He pulls her behind him. The two of them back away. Slowly… slowly…

The scavenger kids edge forward, but Shane keeps his gun trained on them. They don't dare get too close.

Shane and Dawn reach the end of the sideshow aisle. Shane guides her to the left. Shane's truck is parked on the road nearby.

When they reach the truck, Shane gives Dawn a hard look. "I don't kidnap people. If you want a ride home, climb in. Otherwise, you can stay here. Your choice."

Dawn looks back – the scavenger kids are arranged on a ridge of rubble and trash, silhouetted against the low, late-afternoon sun, watching them. A ten-year-old boy absently licks blood from the back of his hand. Dawn shudders.

Shane nods. "Home it is then." He opens the passenger door.

A dog is waiting there, a stocky, black-and-brown mutt.

“Slaughter,” Shane says, “you be nice to this young lady.”

Dawn steps up to the truck – and Slaughter grins, tail wagging. What kind of name is Slaughter for such a cute dog? Dawn reaches to pet him–

“Careful!” Shane warns.

But Slaughter licks Dawn’s hand lovingly.

She smiles. “Guess he likes me.”

“Guess so.”

Dawn climbs into the truck and Shane closes the door. He hurries around to the driver’s side.

Dawn looks out the window. The scavenger kids have crept closer.

Shane slips into his seat, starts the truck, puts it in gear.

He wastes no time in getting the hell out of there.

Chapter 9

Dawn's phone is dead. Submersion in the river was the final blow. These models were supposed to be waterproof, but she cracked the case three months ago when she dropped it on the sidewalk, and as long as the phone worked, her father wouldn't buy her a new one. Prices have gotten outrageous for anything with a microchip in the last couple years. Well, if she can't find a way to give Shane the slip, she'll end up back in Mt. Tucker, and her father will *have* to buy her a new phone. Once he's done punishing her for running away, anyway, which could be months.

Dawn shoves the useless phone in her bag. Maybe she can sell it for parts. Outside the windshield of the truck, the cracked, grey asphalt of the highway winds through undulating hills of pale green pine, broken occasionally by meadows of tall grass dotted with wildflowers. Shane drives silently, barely acknowledging her presence.

Dawn unwraps a piece of gum and pops it in her mouth. Blows a bubble. *POP*. Bats her hands on the dash in time to the old rock song on the radio. Glances at Shane to see his reaction.

Nothing.

This guy is as friendly as a rock.

Dawn cranes her neck around. In the back of the cab is a cramped living area with a narrow bed. Stuff is taped everywhere. “You live back here?”

“Yep.” Shane keeps his eyes fixed on the road.

Dawn undoes her seat belt, climbs back. “Wow, sweet. You got a TV and everything.” The space is small, but kind of cozy. A shelf holds some battered paperbacks and graphic novels. Another is stuffed with folded shirts and jeans. Shane’s used binder clips to hang his wet flannel shirt from the cords holding the shelf contents in place. There’s a column with a small refrigerator, coffee maker, and microwave. Two mugs and a medallion from a marathon hang from hooks next to the coffee maker. A cluster of photographs is taped above the bed. They all portray some combination of Shane, a pretty woman, and a five-year-old boy. “Is this your wife and kid?”

“Yep.”

“You don’t seem like the married type. Where are they?”

“Dead.”

Dawn’s chest tightens. Shit. “I’m sorry. The pandemic?”

“No.”

He doesn’t elaborate.

Dawn slips back into the passenger seat. “Is my dad paying you a lot to bring me back?”

"If I knew how things were going to go, I would've asked for more."

"If my dad had his way, I'd stay in Mount Tucker for the rest of my life."

Shane finally looks at her. "Mount Tucker's safe."

"And boring. What am I supposed to do, just marry Steve Englehoff and start pumping out babies? Dad would love that. He thinks Steve's such a nice boy."

"He's not?"

"No! All the guys in Mount Tucker are self-absorbed, macho jerks. None of them are half as smart as Eric. He has dreams. He has vision. We're in love."

Shane doesn't appear moved by her speech.

"You live out here in the plague zones," Dawn says. "You're not sick."

Shane shrugs. "Been lucky."

"Would you live in Mt. Tucker if you could?"

"Doesn't matter. I can't."

She looks him over. He doesn't look anything like the men in Mt. Tucker. Everyone's had to become a little more self-reliant these days, but Shane has a rugged, unflappable vibe, like he's the kind of guy who just gets the job done, whatever the job is. Dawn shakes her head. "I don't think you would. You get to drive all over, have adventures, see the world."

Shane snorts. "The world's overrated."

"If you take me back, I'll just run away again."

"That's your dad's problem, not mine."

A female voice crackles over the CB. "Breaker two-four, this is La Llorona. Just spotted a burned-out rig at mile 512 of route seventeen. No sign of the driver. Keep your eyes open, boys. I'm 10-10 in the wind."

Dawn examines the handset hanging from the dash. "You guys still use CB's?"

"Yep. Most truckers in this area monitor channel 24." Shane turns onto an access ramp to another highway.

"So, what, you spend all your time driving from town to town through plague zones delivering stuff?"

"Yep."

"And they pay you for that?"

Shane throws her a sidelong look. Clearly losing patience.

"I'm just asking," Dawn protests. "It's a long drive."

"It's sure turning into one."

Dawn folds her arms and stares at him.

Shane relents with a sigh. "Places like Mount Tucker need food, spare parts, stuff for the stores. Can't make everything local."

"Sounds like a lonely job."

"I don't like most people anyway."

"I read online some guy may have found a cure. You hear that?"

"Yep."

"Think it's true?"

Shane just shrugs.

Dawn studies all the switches and dials on the dashboard. Some of them are aftermarket additions. "Is it hard to drive a truck?"

"It's not rocket science."

"How many gears does it have?"

"Since they shifted to electric engines, only two forward gears."

"Can I try it?"

"No."

Dawn thrusts her lips into a pout. "You're not much fun, are you?"

That gets a tiny smile from Shane.

Sunset.

Shane pulls off the highway at the exit for the Pine Ridge Gateway Plaza. The complex consists of a roadhouse, fuel station, travel store, and motel, all surrounded by a high, razor wire-topped fence and lit by blinding arc lights. The vast parking lot is half full of cars and several long rows of big rigs.

Shane guides his truck through the gate, waving at the guard, who nods in return. Based on who the complex lets in, Shane can't imagine who gets turned away.

"What are we doing?" Dawn asks.

"The battery's low, and I'm hungry. Thanks to you, I missed breakfast *and* lunch. Besides, it's dangerous to drive these roads at night."

Recharging the truck is the first priority. Shane pulls up to a charging station and puts on his facemask. "Stay here. And don't mess with anything."

Dawn gives him a dirty look, crosses her arms, and slouches down in the passenger seat.

After hooking up the charging cable, Shane returns to the cab and gets Slaughter's leash from the pocket by the door. "Come on boy."

Slaughter hops out.

Dawn sits forward, curious. "What are you doing?"

"He needs a walk."

"Can I do it?"

It's the first time Shane's seen the girl without a scowl on her face. "Sure. There's a grassy area over there." He points to a strip of greenspace at the edge of the lot. "Just clean up after him. There are bags in the leash handle. And don't go outside the fence."

Shane does an inspection of the truck. Despite the day's adventures, it seems mostly undamaged. When he has a chance, he'll have to get an alignment and check the shocks and struts. That drop off the ferry was pretty gnarly. He shudders as the image flashes in his mind.

Dawn returns with Slaughter, a big grin plastered across her face. The dog looks pretty happy as well. Dawn hands Shane the leash and crouches down to scratch behind Slaughter's ear. "I always wanted a dog, but my mom wouldn't let us have one. She said they get hair everywhere and pee on everything."

Shane laughs. "Well, she's not wrong about the hair." He ties Slaughter to the bumper of the truck and puts his water and food dishes in reach. He gives the dog a good head rub.

Slaughter is proving useful in unexpected ways on this job.

The roadhouse is dim – wood paneled, wagon wheel "chandeliers," sawdust floor. A house band plays country-tinged hard rock on stage. The clientele ranges from badass to psychopath. They drink, play pool, dance, pass out. Shane fits right in. Dawn sticks out like an erection on a priest.

They sit at a table near the dance floor. Dawn looks around wide-eyed, clearly enjoying herself. "This place is awesome."

Shane picks up a menu. "I never heard it called that, but the burgers aren't bad."

The waitress comes over. She has bright purple hair and wears a matching purple flannel shirt over a red crop top. Her facemask and face shield are bedazzled with purple rhinestones. "What'll y'all have?"

"Give me a cheeseburger and whatever IPA you have on tap," Shane says.

Dawn nods. "Same."

"Except she'll have a Coke instead of a beer," Shane says.

Dawn glares at Shane for a moment, then looks up at the waitress. "*Diet* Coke, please."

The waitress leaves, and Dawn turns her chair so she can see the stage. "The band kinda rocks. You want to dance?"

"No."

She gives him puppy dog eyes. "Come on, what are you afraid of?"

"Dancing."

"Well, I want to dance."

"Knock yourself out. Just stay close, keep your mask on, and try to maintain a little social distance. This isn't Mt. Tucker."

Dawn scampers to the dance floor and finds an empty spot. She begins moving to the music. Not just moving – bumping and grinding. She must've picked up a thing or two from music videos. Suddenly, she doesn't look so young. Her father may be able to keep her in Mt. Tucker, but sooner or later he's going to have to come to terms with the fact that she's growing up.

That's not Shane's problem, though. He checks the news feeds on his phone.

The waitress brings their food. Dawn can dance the night away if she wants, Shane's hungry. He removes his mask and takes a big bite of his burger. It's juicy, medium rare, topped with a nice, sharp cheddar and lots of pickles – just the way he likes it.

La Llorona and Sheik come up to the table. La Llorona is a lanky Latina with long, dark hair, dressed all in black. She gets her moniker from a teardrop birthmark under her right eye. Sheik is a stout Arab with a bushy salt-and-pepper mustache who favors western wear.

"Hot girl, Kodiak," La Llorona says. "Where'd you find her?"

"She's a job."

Sheik grins. "Really? Sign me up."

Shane rolls his eyes. "I'm just taking her back to Mount Tucker."

La Llorona slips into Dawn's chair, steals one of her fries. "We're headed to Ashford tomorrow if you want to convoy."

"Yeah, cool." For the first time since the ferry, Shane relaxes a little. A convoy will make the drive a lot safer. He takes a swig of his IPA.

Sheik nods toward the dance floor. "Hey, looks like someone's moving in on your job."

Sure enough, a road worker – big and muscled, still wearing his brown, state issue canvas jacket and reflective facemask – has sidled up to Dawn. She doesn't seem to mind. In fact, she's bumping and grinding on him pretty good.

La Llorona laughs. "Bet you wish you'd agreed to dance with her now."

Shane shakes his head. "The girl's got more curves than brains."

"My kind of girl," Sheik says.

La Llorona nudges Shane under the table with her foot. "She's just having fun. You should try it – you might like it."

Sheik nods toward Dawn again. "Looks like he missed his chance."

The road worker leads Dawn off the dance floor, an arm around her waist. They head for a hallway with a sign for the restrooms.

"Ah, hell." Shane drops his burger and goes after them.

Shane finds Dawn and the road worker glued together in a dark corner where the payphone used to be. Dawn's sucking on a beer bottle. The road worker is feeling her ass.

Shane sighs. “Enough screwing around, Dawn. Let’s go.”

She snorts. “Fuck off.”

“I don’t know what you’re up to, but it’s been a really long day.”

The road worker glances at Shane. Then, to Dawn, “Who is this guy?”

“Just some creep who won’t leave me alone.”

Now the road worker meets Shane’s gaze. Evenly. Ice cold. “You heard the lady, buddy. Fuck off.”

Shane tries to do it the easy way. “She’s playing you, man. Why don’t you go back to the bar and get another beer? On me.”

The road worker releases Dawn, squares off against Shane. “You’re not listening.”

Shane peers around the burly man at Dawn. “You are so not worth this.”

“I think you need to learn some manners,” the road worker growls. He shoves Shane.

So much for the easy way.

Dawn sticks her tongue out at Shane as she slips out a back door – unnoticed by the road worker.

The road worker balls up his fist, yells, “Jose! Kyle!”

Two other road workers appear behind Shane. Both as big as the first.

“This guy was rude to my lady,” the first road worker explains.

“What lady?” one of the newcomers asks.

The first road worker spins to find Dawn gone. He turns back to Shane with a furious growl. “Should have minded your own business, asshole.”

Okay, maybe not logical, but there's no point wasting time arguing logic with a trio of drunk brutes. It's clear where this is going, and if Shane doesn't want to spend the night in the hospital, he better make a preemptive strike.

He kicks back, takes out Road Worker Two's knee.

Spins – roundhouse to Road Worker Three–

But the element of surprise is gone. The first road worker grabs Shane, lifts him off the ground, hurls him into the main dining area. Shane *CRASHES* into a table, sending dirty dishes flying. Pain lances through his shoulder.

He rolls off the table, landing on his feet. The three road workers emerge from the hallway.

La Llorona and Sheik step up beside Shane. "Looks like you decided to have some fun after all," Sheik observes.

The road workers charge – the brawl is on.

DAWN

Runs from the roadhouse across the vast parking lot as the *thumps* and *tinkles* of shattering glass from a major bar fight punctuate the rock beat from inside. The night is getting cool. She shivers.

She reaches the truck. Releases Slaughter from his leash. "Go on. Get out of here."

The dog grins up at her, tail thumping the pavement.

"Okay, whatever."

She holds up the fob she lifted from Shane's jacket pocket while he was ordering their food and presses the button.

Chirp.

She climbs on the running board and opens the truck's driver side door. Punches the release button for the charging port.

She hops down and disconnects the charging cable.

When she steps back up to the driver's door, she discovers Slaughter sitting on the passenger seat, panting happily at her.

Whatever. Dawn climbs into the driver's seat, closes the door, and starts the engine.

SHANE

Bursts out of the roadhouse in time to see Dawn pull his truck out of the parking spot. He hauls ass after her.

CRUNCH!

The truck clips a light pole as it rumbles out of the gate. Shane cringes. The armor plating over the front wheel took the brunt of the blow, so the pole got the worst of it, but if that girl puts another scratch on his vehicle, he'll be tempted to sell her to the river pirates himself.

Dawn turns the truck onto the highway, heading South, away from Mt. Tucker. Shane pulls up at the gate of the travel center, panting. He flexes his hands, his knuckles aching from the punches he landed inside.

La Llorona saunters up.

Shane turns to her. "The little bitch stole my truck!"

La Llorona raises an eyebrow. "She may not be as dumb as you think she is."

Shane scowls at La Llorona.

Chapter 10

Bones and the Piranhaz have circled their vehicles in a vacant parking lot across the street from the Renton ferry terminal. Most of the gangsters are dozing as the sun rises above the eastern hills. Bones sits on the hood of the red Mustang, savoring a grande drip he got from the local Starbucks. Nobody makes decent coffee back at the Piranhaz' base camp.

It's been a long and uncomfortable night sleeping in the cars. The ferry did not arrive on schedule. The Piranhaz didn't panic, just used the delay as an excuse for an impromptu party. But as evening turned to night, Bones started to suspect something had gone very wrong. At sunrise, he finally sent Rainbow to the terminal office to see what was up.

Rainbow jogs back across the street, wincing as her wounded arm bounces in its sling. "The ferry was hit by pirates upriver," she gasps.

Just as Bones feared. "Survivors?"

Rainbow pops a generic opioid into her mouth, swallows. "Some."

Bones scowls. There's a good chance pirates wouldn't do a very thorough search of the vehicles. They probably didn't find super trucker's stash. But if super trucker is dead, getting access to his vehicle will be more complicated. Not to mention the Piranhaz would be denied the opportunity for revenge for all the trouble he's caused them.

Rainbow climbs up beside him. "They're towing the ferry in. It should be here in a couple hours."

Bones sips his coffee and begins planning how they're going to get onto the ferry when it arrives.

In the morning light filtering through the small, grimy windows, the roadhouse seems particularly dingy. A scattering of patrons eat their breakfasts in silence. Shane sits by himself, nursing a coffee and a black eye.

La Llorona and Sheik come by. "Sorry we can't help you get your truck back," La Llorona says, "but we're hauling perishables."

Shane nods. "That's okay."

"We get into Ashford tonight, and then I'm free for a couple days. Call me if you still need help."

"Thanks, L."

Sheik puts an encouraging hand on Shane's shoulder. "Good luck, Kodiak." He and La Llorona head out.

Shane can't blame them – they've got their jobs to do. He's used to solving his own problems. Only, without transportation, this one's going to be a challenge. Dawn was meeting her boyfriend in Renton. If she drove all night, she could be there already. But what were her plans after that? Maybe he should have talked to her more when he had the chance.

A man enters the roadhouse who's known to everyone simply as Preacher. He's a tall, strapping Black guy with a leather biker jacket and a big, gold cross around his neck. His black N95 mask sports the word, "LOVE" in big, white letters. He goes to the bar. "A dozen coffees to go, please."

The waitress nods acknowledgement.

This may be the solution Shane is looking for. He puts on his face mask and slides up next to Preacher. "'Morning."

"Hey, Shane."

Preacher's eyes are fixed on the TV mounted high on the wall of the bar. On screen, Reverend Elliot is in full fire and brimstone mode: "...I want you to think back to the first time the plague hit close to your home. Did you pray for God to spare you? Did you beg for his protection? Well, now it's time to pay God back. God's asking for something from you. He's asking for money to support His great works. So, I want you to think about how scared you were when you said those prayers and send whatever you think you might owe God for sparing your life to the address on your screen..."

Preacher turns away. "Asshole. He lives in a clean-zone mansion and has limousines for his bodyguards while we've got people starving to death out here."

"Which way you headed this morning, Preacher?" Shane asks.

"South."

"Think I could hitch a ride to Renton?"

"Of course, if you don't mind a few stops. I still owe you for Ohio. But what happened to your truck?"

"Long story."

Dawn applies fuchsia lipstick to go with her pink sweater and skirt combo. She steps back to survey the results and bumps into the wall. The truck's bathroom is ridiculously tiny.

She feels another pang of regret for her lost mane of golden hair, but she's spiked her new, short hair into a flirty, punkish 'do. It's cuter than she would have expected. Hopefully, Eric will feel the same. She was a kid last time they saw each other in person. They've exchanged a bazillion photos, but she knows all the tricks to taking a good selfie. What if he's disappointed in the real, no-filter Dawn?

She shakes it off. Eric's not like that. That's why she's leaving Mt. Tucker in the first place. Eric and she have a deeper connection. He understands how trapped she's felt. He understands that she wants more out of life. He does, too. Sure, a lot of the world has gone to hell since the last pandemic hit, but together they can face anything. Together, maybe they can even change the world. Isn't that what love is, after all?

She exits the bathroom. Slaughter's waiting for her. He whimpers and nudges his bowl with his nose.

Dawn finds a bag of dogfood in one of the cabinets. She fills the bowl – she's unsure how much food is appropriate, never having owned a dog, but Slaughter's pretty big. As he attacks his breakfast, Dawn smooths the blanket on the small bed. She slept on top of the sheets, but it was too cold to sleep above the blanket. The little bed was too hard, and the pillow smelled a bit funky, but none of that kept her awake.

Dawn slides into the driver's seat. Slaughter jumps up into the passenger seat beside her. She parked the truck on a tree-shaded turnout on a rural road just off the highway when she got too tired to drive last night.

She starts the engine, pulls out onto the road. Scans the landscape. The glass in the driver-side window is pocked and cracked. The truck has been through some things. Dawn feels a little bad for Shane. He could obviously use the money her dad was going to pay him. Then again, Dawn's pretty broke herself at the moment.

She checks her mirrors. Still nobody around. Thank goodness.

She heads for the highway entrance ramp.

The ferry has been towed in and tied up at the Renton Ferry Terminal, the survivors evacuated, the injured taken to the hospital, all questioned by the local police – who will simply make reports to the Federal authorities, who, in turn, will spend more time debating priorities in light of their rapidly vanishing budget than they will putting a stop to the river pirates.

Bones has patiently observed this process play out from the driver seat of the Mustang parked in the shade of a building half a block away. Rainbow is in the passenger seat. She has been less patient and is starting to get on Bones' nerves with her constant chatter and restless fidgeting. Maria, Tyler, Mouse, and Carlos are playing poker in a grey Tesla Model 3 behind them. The railroad spikes welded haphazardly all over the Tesla's body might draw attention, but its neutral color helps it blend into the surroundings. Bones has sent the rest of the Piranhaz off looking for opportunities to swipe supplies. This is a stealth mission. He needs people who can keep their heads.

Finally, the activity at the ferry has mostly subsided. Only a smattering of guards patrols the terminal area. Bones opens the door. "Let's go."

Bones, Rainbow, Maria, and Mouse lope across the street. It would be better to do this in the middle of the night, but Bones doesn't want to risk the vehicles left on the ferry being taken to a more secure location. Tyler and Carlos head to the empty lot across from the terminal to provide the distraction.

Bones and his three compatriots hop the terminal fence between a shed and a pile of rotting timbers. They creep through the terminal yard, find cover behind a forklift parked a dozen feet from the ferry ramp.

Tyler and Carlos start their show. They argue loudly – something about one of them sleeping with the other's girl. It's all improvised, of course. Tyler isn't even into girls.

Bones checks the guards. All are focused on the ruckus across the street. But one stands on the ferry at the end of the ramp. They won't be able to get by him without being spotted. Bones nods to Maria.

Maria unslings the small crossbow from her back. Nocks an arrow. Takes aim. Hits the trigger.

The arrow pierces the guard's throat.

The guard's mouth opens, but no sound comes out. He collapses to his knees, then down on his face.

Bones checks the other guards. They're all still watching the action in the lot.

That action now involves Tyler and Carlos pulling their guns. When the terminal guards see this, they scramble for cover. That's the cue for Bones' party to make their move.

As Tyler and Carlos fire wildly at everything but each other, Bones, Rainbow, Mouse, and Maria scramble across the ramp to the ferry.

Once onboard, things get easier. The ferry is deserted. The four gangsters walk among the cars on the auto deck, stepping over patches of dried blood.

They reconvene at the far end of the garage deck. "Where the hell is his truck?" Bones growls.

"I don't think it's here," Rainbow replies.

Bones smashes the side of his fist onto the hood of a Range Rover, leaving a dent. "How could it not be here? We saw him drive on. There were no stops before this. Where the hell could he go in the middle of a river?"

Rainbow can only shrug.

Chapter 11

Shane rides in the passenger seat of the lead car of Preacher's convoy, a platinum Cadillac Lyriq with a black cross painted on the hood and a machine gun mounted on the roof above Shane's head, the weapon's controls on the dash in front of him. Even a man of God like Preacher has to be able to defend himself in post-pandemic rural America. If trouble comes, though, Preacher would probably be glad to have Shane be the one doling out the violence. The rest of the convoy trails behind, two box trucks, a van, and a couple more cars protecting the rear.

Preacher is rambling on in his booming voice about a recent city election in Detroit. A slate backed by a coalition of automotive corporations won and is clashing with the federal government. It may be an important development, but Shane's been too busy with his own problems to worry about politics. Currently, his main problem is getting his truck back. He replays everything Dawn said, trying to find a clue as to where she might be going.

Preacher seems to sense Shane's disinterest. "How 'bout you, Shane? You doing okay?"

Shane snorts. "If I was doing okay, I wouldn't need to hitch a ride with you."

"I wasn't talking about the worldly stuff. How are you doing in here?" Preacher smacks a fist into Shane's chest above his heart.

"I'm hanging in there."

"Want to talk about it?"

"Not really."

"Might help."

It's tempting. Preacher has a way of getting people to open up. You feel safe with him. But if Shane starts talking about the crushing grief buried deep in his heart, it's liable to overwhelm him, and then he won't be able to focus on the task at hand. "I'm fine. Really."

"I'm here if you need me." Preacher puts a hand on Shane's forearm, gives it a squeeze. "These people who stole your truck, are they dangerous?"

Shane actually laughs at that. "No. She's not dangerous. Annoying, self-involved, and reckless maybe, but not dangerous."

The convoy diverts off the highway to a small farm town nestled in a valley. It looks to be about three quarters abandoned. They pass a house that has been gutted by fire and not cleaned up, streaks of black char staining the blistered yellow paint above the windows and doors. Large black Xs are spray painted on the doors of many other houses, an indication that the occupants are all deceased. The faint but pungent odor of manure wafts from the surrounding fields.

Preacher's convoy parks in the middle of a trash-strewn street. Preacher pulls on his N95 mask and a face shield and gets out. Shane puts on his own mask and follows.

Preacher's congregation – an eclectic collection of young hippies and middle-aged women, gather at the back of one of the box trucks where a skinny, older Black man hands out latex gloves.

Shane steps up to take a pair of gloves. Preacher gives him a nod of gratitude.

Once they've donned their protective gear, the congregants take boxes and bags from the truck and fan out by twos to the houses without X marks.

Shane grabs a bag. Inside are staple foods – flour, oil, peanut butter, and cans of beans, vegetables, and soup.

"Shane," Preacher calls, "with me."

They go to a small, green house, the flower bed along the front overgrown with weeds. A skinny, pale woman in threadbare sweats opens the door before they reach it.

"Morning, Anna," Preacher says, his voice cheerful. "Good to see you again. How have you folks been faring?"

The woman sighs. "I'd be lying if I said we were good. We had another outbreak. Six people died since you been here last."

Preacher shakes his head. "Sorry to hear that."

"Molly Shaker and Juan Mendoza are still pretty bad off. The rest of us, we're figuring to pool our labor and harvest the most productive fields if we can. Don't know if any seasonal workers will come through this year, but we ain't got nothing to give them if they do."

"We're all just doing the best we can," Preacher says, "and that's all anyone can ask of us. Keep the faith, Anna. I'll pray for you."

Shane hands Anna the bag. He can tell she's smiling by the way the edges of her bloodshot eyes crinkle above her mask.

"Thank you," she whispers. "Thank you so much."

Preacher waves his goodbye. "We'll be back through in another month or so."

Preacher and Shane head back to the truck to get another load. Preacher is uncharacteristically quiet.

"You think there'll be anyone left here in another month?" Shane asks.

"Starvation we can fight, but this disease…" Preacher shakes his head. "I've seen miracles even in the darkest times. All we can do is keep on keeping on."

Shane grunts. Preacher's right about that.

Rainbow drives the Mustang at the head of the Piranhaz' convoy as they make their way back north on the highway.

Bones fumes in the passenger seat beside her. "What a fucking waste of time. This trucker is starting to piss me off."

Rainbow's been pissed off at the trucker for a long time now, but unfortunately the opportunity for revenge might have passed. “The pirates probably killed him. He would have fought.”

Bones shakes his head. “It still doesn't make sense. How would they get his truck off the ferry? Where the hell is that truck?”

As if on cue, then they see a bright red truck cab approaching from the opposite direction.

It has a bear claw symbol on the door.

Their heads swivel in unison as it passes. The trucker is not behind the wheel. Some teenage girl with short, spiky hair peers out at the road.

“Who the hell is that?” Rainbow says. “She doesn't look like a pirate.”

“Who cares,” Bones growls, “turn the fuck around!”

She can't though. There's a cement median barrier. Rainbow hits the gas, takes the next exit. The rest of the Piranhaz’ vehicles follow her.

The truck is more difficult to drive than Dawn expected. It’s so big and responds so slowly. But she must be getting close to Renton. A convoy of armored vehicles passes on the other side of the highway, the most people she’s seen in miles.

She rounds a bend and spots the sign she’s been looking for:

Renton Zoo - Next Exit

She guides the truck onto the exit ramp. Her heart is pounding. She's finally going to see Eric.

The cluster of restaurants and convenience stores by the exit ramp are dark, their lots empty. The zoo is about two miles from the freeway. Dawn drives under the arched zoo sign, no attendant to collect the posted parking fee. Brings the truck to a halt in the middle of the vast lot. No other cars here, either.

Dawn checks her makeup in the mirror on the visor. There's a picture clipped there of Shane and his family posing stiffly by a barbecue grill. The boy appears to be about ten and is wearing a party hat. A pang of guilt pierces Dawn's excitement. She flips the visor back up.

Dawn opens the glove box and removes the pistol she discovered when she searched the truck. She slides it in her purse. She's never fired a gun, but it makes her feel safer. She pulls out her facemask but doesn't put it on. There's nobody around here to infect her. She climbs out of the truck.

The zoo is small, a local attraction. A hand painted banner across the entrance says: "Closed." Dawn peers through the locked gate. An old potato chip bag blows across the path. It's a ghost town.

"Eric?" she shouts.

No response.

What now? Eric should have gotten there long before this. How long does she wait?

Then – a *rustling* to her left.

She retrieves Shane's gun from her purse.

"Dawn?" It's Eric. He emerges from the brush. He's skinny, delicate featured, his curly brown hair overdue for a trim, a panicked look in his big eyes. Gorgeous. Vulnerable.

Dawn breathes a sigh of relief and lowers the gun. “Eric!”

Love wells up in her so powerfully that her chest feels like it’s going to explode. She runs to him, throws her arms around him, kisses him.

She’s imagined this for months, lying awake late into the night, staring at his picture, thinking about him taking her in his arms. Her whole body tingles.

He breaks the kiss, squeezes her to him, oh so tight.

He gasps in a long, ragged breath. His chest heaves against her.

She steps back. He’s crying.

She takes his hand. “What's wrong?”

“I thought you were dead. I didn't know what to do. You were supposed to be here last night.”

“I had problems on the ferry. I told you I might not make it 'til this morning.”

“I texted you like a dozen times. I almost called your parents!”

He’s really freaked out. She hugs him again. “My phone got wet. Calm down, I'm here now.”

He pulls away. Gestures toward the zoo. “Look at this place, Dawn! It was my favorite place when we were kids. Now it's ruined. I snuck in.... They just left the animals there to die! I think some might have escaped.” His eyes dart instinctively side-to-side.

What was his night like here all alone? Maybe it’s better not to ask. “I guess the zoo wasn't a high priority after the pandemic.”

He shakes his head. “It's so much worse out here than I thought.”

“I know. Come on, let's go somewhere where there's people.”

Dawn takes surface streets into town. There’s lots of green space out here, now overgrown and wild-looking. They pass a large outlet mall, apparently vacant and looted, half-dressed mannequins piled in front of broken windows. The streets are dotted with mostly deserted businesses and scattered clusters of houses, even a few that still look occupied. It’s quiet, sunny, still. Strangely pleasant if you can ignore the implications of that stillness.

Slaughter stands between the seats, staring down Eric with a low, rumbling *growl.*

“Slaughter, be nice,” Dawn orders.

Slaughter quits growling. Keeps glaring.

Eric shifts nervously. “Is he yours?”

“No, he belongs to... a friend.”

“Is this your friend's truck, too?”

“Yeah, I sort of borrowed it. I'm gonna have to give it back.”

Dawn checks the mirror and is surprised to see the convoy she saw earlier on the highway a few blocks behind them. What are they doing here? The back of her neck tingles with apprehension.

The convoy is closing… fast.

Chapter 12

The lead car of the convoy swerves into the oncoming traffic lane and pulls parallel to Dawn's window. It's a red Mustang plastered with stickers. A crude symbol of a flat-faced fish is painted on the side of the door. The driver of the car is a woman with a rainbow mohawk. The passenger is a guy with his bones tattooed on his arms, hands, and bald head... every visible part of his skin.

The bald dude motions for Dawn to pull over. Her stomach goes queasy. What now?

"Who are those guys?" Eric asks.

"No clue." Dawn adjusts her grip on the wheel. She's clenching it so tightly her fingers ache.

Eric rubs his forehead. "Maybe we should pull over."

"I don't think that's a very good idea."

The bald guy motions more emphatically. A grey Tesla bristling with spikes pulls up on the passenger side of the truck, driving in the parking lane.

The bald guy gets frustrated, points a big, shiny pistol at Dawn.

Dawn *squeaks*, jams her foot on the gas – the truck lurches forward. But it can't out-accelerate the Mustang.

The bald guy runs out of patience – pulls the trigger–

BLAM–

Dawn *screams–*

THUNK–

The bullet bounces off the window, leaving another divot of circular cracks.

Dawn lets out a shaky gasp. The glass must be bulletproof. That's what the other divots are – former bullet strikes. No harm done, except maybe to her panties.

And to her control of the truck.

The scare made her jerk the wheel impulsively – the truck swerves – she corrects – too much – the truck *CRUNCHES* into the Tesla to her right – sends it spinning into a parking lot.

The Mustang brakes, slides back to avoid the wildly careening truck.

Dawn manages to regain control. Kind of. "Ohmigod, omigod, omigod!"

Eric hyperventilates. "They shot at us!"

"I know!"

"Dawn, get us out of here!"

"I'm trying!"

She jams the wheel left – *SCREECHES* around a corner – nearly sending the truck over. But her brain's working again. She grabs the CB handset. "Hello, hello? Can anyone hear me? Shane, are you out there?"

Preacher's convoy has stopped on the outskirts of Renton to recharge the vehicles in a little pocket of town where survivors have condensed for safety. Shane washes the windows of Preacher's Cadillac while it sucks volts from a charging station. He's going to have to part ways with the convoy and start his search for the truck soon, maybe when they reach downtown. Would Dawn and her boyfriend head toward or away from the densest population? How would sheltered, pandemic-era teenagers think?

And then Dawn's voice crackles over the Caddy's CB. "Hello, hello? Can anyone hear me? Shane, are you out there?"

Shane grabs the handset through the window. "Dawn, is that you? Over."

"I need help! A gang or something is chasing us. They tried to make us crash!"

The Piranhaz. "What's your 20? Over."

"What?"

Shane takes a deep breath. "Where are you?"

"Um... West Park Drive in Renton. We just crossed Oak. Heading west."

"Okay, I'm close. Keep moving. I'm on my way. Out."

He clicks off. Turns to Preacher. "Uh, Preacher–"

Preacher tosses Shane the car's key fob. "Try to return it in one piece."

Dawn zigzags across the road, keeping the gangsters behind her, going as fast as she dares. The truck leans dangerously as it swerves. They fly through a red light. Fortunately, nobody else is out and about in this part of town.

Eric's watching the passenger mirror. “Two cars turned off!”

Dawn glances back. A Jeep Cherokee and a bright yellow Volkswagen ID.4 vanish up a side street. The red Mustang is close on her tail, and behind that the spiked Tesla has rejoined the chase, sparks flying from a front side panel dragging on the asphalt. There are also half a dozen motorcycles scattered across the road. One of them edges up on her left.

Dawn jerks the wheel that way, and the motorcycle falls back, but the truck sways ominously from the sudden movement. Dawn’s stomach clenches. Man, Shane better get here fast.

They approach a major intersection – abandoned fast food joints and strip malls on the corners. Ahead and to the right, the Jeep and the VW careen around onto the cross street. They’re maneuvering to cut her off, and if she continues on her current path, they’ll succeed. Could the truck punch through the cars? Probably, but what if a tire blows? And there’s a big machine gun mounted on the hood of the Cherokee. Big enough, maybe, to get through the truck’s bulletproof gas.

Avoidance seems the better option. Dawn veers into a fast-food drive through – going the wrong way – *CRUNCH* – the truck obliterates the microphone kiosk. A picture of a decadent triple burger with chili momentarily plasters itself to the windshield before blowing off behind her.

She *screeches* out onto the cross street – still going the wrong way. A tree-lined median separates the lanes.

Eric grabs the dash with both hands. “You're driving on the left side of the street!”

Dawn tears her eyes from the road just long enough to give him a withering look. “*That's* what you're worried about?”

“I don't know – this is my first car chase!”

At least the median separates them from the two cars that were trying to cut them off. But a check of the side mirror shows the Mustang, Tesla, and motorcycles have followed them into the wrong-way lanes.

Shane’s voice comes over the CB. “Breaker two-four for Dawn. You out there, Dawn?”

Dawn grabs the handset. “Yeah. I'm here.”

“Where, exactly?”

She looks around. “I have no idea!”

“Do you see a water tower?”

Eric points ahead and to the right. “There it is!”

Dawn spots the water tower protruding above the surrounding buildings a few miles away. She depresses the button on the CB handset. “I see it.”

“Head toward it,” Shane instructs. “I'll find you.”

Dawn makes a hard right at the next intersection.

RAINBOW

Grins. She and Bones have been listening in on the conversation via their own CB. “Looks like Super Trucker is about to join the party.”

Shane pulls Preacher's Cadillac to a stop next to the water tower and gets out. He's atop a low hill overlooking a seemingly deserted industrial area – warehouses, sagging factories, train tracks, etc. He can see his truck approaching on the main road below – maybe three miles away now. The Piranhaz are hot on its tail. He's got to find some way to impede the pursuit so he can get back in his truck.

Shane opens the Caddy's trunk. It's packed with tools, fuel cans, rope. He spots a chainsaw.

Bingo.

Rainbow stays patient. As the truck weaves back and forth, she weaves with it, waiting for her chance.

Bones points to something up ahead. "What's that?"

Rainbow swerves to the left so she can see around the truck. Super trucker is on the side of the road up ahead – sawing into a wooden power pole with a chainsaw.

"Ah, shit!" Rainbow hits the brakes–

The trucker cuts deep into the pole as the truck approaches – *CRACK* – the pole leans – falls – just misses the truck–

And *CRASHES* onto the hood of Rainbow's skidding Mustang, crushing the front end.

The airbags blow – pain lances through Rainbow's nose. Her wounded shoulder screams.

Power lines whip through the air with a bell-like *whistle* before settling to the pavement.

The other Piranhaz *screech* to a stop behind them. The trucker takes off.

Rainbow grabs the AR-5 from the floor behind her. Wrenches the door open. It jams halfway. She squeezes through the gap, stumbles out.

The trucker bolts into a four-foot-diameter drainage pipe. Rainbow opens fire.

TAT-TAT-TAT-TAT!

Too late. The trucker is gone.

Bones climbs out of the wrecked Mustang, spitting blood. He lopes for the closest Piranhaz car, the yellow ID.4. "Forget that asshole. The money's in the truck."

But Rainbow can't forget that damn, troublemaking trucker. She takes off after him, on foot, into the drainage pipe.

DAWN

and Eric draw in deep breaths, letting the adrenaline subside. Dawn careens around a corner. Checks the side mirrors. None of the gangsters are in sight. The downed power pole has bought her some time. She makes another turn at random.

That was close. Who knows why the gang was targeting her or what they had planned, but it couldn't have been good. If Shane hadn't gotten there when he did… maybe she overestimated her ability to survive out he–

A fluffy brown rabbit runs across the road.

Dawn *squeals* – jerks the wheel–

Too much. The truck careens off the road – through a chain link fence – *CRUNCH* – into a junkyard–

Dawn squeezes the truck between two enormous piles of rusted appliances, miraculously misses a stack of rusty pipes–

But not the pointy hunk of metal on the ground. *BANG* – her left front tire blows out. The truck veers hard that direction, slides to a stop in the midst of the junk, a cloud of dust settling around it.

Dawn catches her breath. Looks around. They're in the middle of huge stacks of debris.

She opens the door, slides out.

"Everything okay?" Eric calls from the passenger seat, his voice squeaky with fear and adrenaline.

"The tire's flat." Dawn is calm. A flat tire. They can fix that.

And then she hears tires *screeching* back on the road. A lot of tires.

"They're coming!" She bolts into the warren of junk, panic coursing through her body.

Eric jumps out, follows her, not bothering to close the door.

Rainbow emerges from the drainage pipe on the other side of an earthen berm. It's an industrial ghost town. No sign of the trucker or anyone else. She readies her AR-5. Stalks along the berm.

Gravel *crunches* – from a lot up on top of a low hill where the water tower is perched. Rainbow charges up the slope toward the sound.

The trucker is pulling a Cadillac Lyriq out from behind a row of graffiti-covered bulldozers.

Rainbow opens fire – *TAT-TAT-TAT-TAT!*

Bullets *shatter* the back window – but the Cadillac skids around a building and is gone.

Rainbow unleashes a primal *scream*, fires a burst angrily into the air.

And a moment later a pigeon falls at her feet, shredded by her wild shots. Rainbow yelps and skitters away from the avian carcass.

Dawn and Eric make their way through a complex of hulking warehouses and workshops. Everything is grey, dusty, the air thick with the scent of motor oil and rubber. Dawn spots a coyote running between two buildings, but there is no sign of other people. This whole area must be abandoned.

"Dawn, I think we made a big mistake," Eric whispers.

"What do you mean?"

"Look around! Everything out here is going to hell. Random psychos are chasing us. This isn't how we planned it."

She stops. Turns to him. Takes his hands. "I know. But we're together. Isn't that what's important?" She stares into his big, beautiful eyes.

Eric looks down, doesn't respond.

"Isn't it? Eric?"

"I want to go home, Dawn."

A knot tightens in her belly. "We can't."

"It hasn't been that long. If we go right now, maybe they'll let us back in." The hopeful look in his eyes borders on insanity.

"That's not the point. You said the clean zones are traps. That we can't live our lives in a bubble."

"That was before... all this."

There's a *screech* behind them. They look back to see the yellow ID.4 turning into the alley, bearing down on them. The rest of the gangster convoy is right behind it.

And that crazed hope fades from Eric's eyes. Replaced by terror. "Oh no… oh no…"

"This way!" Dawn pulls him toward the nearest building.

Dawn and Eric scramble into a barn-like train repair hanger. Dawn latches the door. Eric hyperventilates. He's losing it.

Dawn spots a bin of metal rebar nearby. She tries to push it toward the door. It weighs a ton. "Eric, help me!"

Eric shakes off his panic, joins her. The bin scrapes along the concrete floor. They slowly inch it toward the door.

The door latch jiggles – the gangsters have reached it.

A moment later – *BANG* – something hits the door hard from the other side. Eric squeals, "They're going to get through!"

Dawn leans her full bodyweight against the bin. "Keep pushing!"

BANG!

The door buckles.

Eric lets go of the bin... edges backward.

Dawn throws herself at the bin, but it won't budge… and it's still two yards from the door. "Eric, what are you doing?"

His answer is to dash for an interior door on the other side of the room.

"Eric!"

BANG – Another blow to the exterior door.

Dawn strains against the bin, her running shoes slipping on the dusty floor. *SCRAPE* – the bin moves two inches. But without Eric, it's hopeless.

She gives up on the bin – runs for the interior door – but trips on a loose jumble of barbed wire.

She tries to free herself, but the barbed wire is wrapped tightly around her ankle. "Eric, help!"

Eric stands in the open interior door. He looks back at her, eyes wild with fear.

CRASH – the exterior door gives – A stocky gangster with headphones around his neck stumbles in, the tattooed guy and a small, wiry guy right behind.

And that does it. Eric steps through the interior doorway.

And closes the door behind him.

Dawn's heart sinks. Did Eric actually just ditch her?

Dawn grits her teeth, yanks her leg free – the barbs tear some nasty gashes in her smooth, pretty ankle.

She ignores the stinging pain – leaps to her feet – dashes for the interior door–

The lead gangster, the one with the headphones, sprints after her–

She reaches the interior door, grabs the handle–

Locked.

"Eric!" She pounds on the door.

But the gangster's right there – grabs her by the throat – spins her and *SLAMS* her back against the door.

ERIC

Cringes at the thumps coming from beyond the door.

He's standing in a tiny office, mostly filled by a battered desk and metal filing cabinet. An outdated calendar on the wall shows a horse-faced woman splayed against a stack of tires, her surgically enhanced breasts positioned to guide the eye to the brand name on one of the sidewalls.

Behind the desk is a window.

Eric looks out. An alley. Empty.

Dawn *cries out* from the other side of the door.

Eric swallows hard. That's his girlfriend who's being manhandled by those thugs. He should help her.

But instead, he opens the window and climbs out.

Chapter 13

Shane drives the Lyriq in the direction Dawn was heading, scanning the side streets. He doesn't want to use the CB to contact her now that he knows the Piranhaz are listening in, but his truck seems to have vanished.

A trio of people scamper across an alley from one building to another. Shane brakes, but they are only scavengers, clothes dirty, hair clumped in greasy strands, hauling bags of pilfered tools and parts. Shane continues down the street.

He hits a dead end at the rail yard. Smacks the steering wheel, whispers a curse. He turns right, circles a large junkyard, backtracks a block to the north. The lots in the industrial area are so big… he may have lost Dawn for a second time.

BARKING – somewhere to his right.

Shane skids to a halt. Rolls down his window.

More *barks*. There must be dozens of stray dogs in the area, but these barks are familiar.

Shane pulls into the right lane, edges the car forward, trying to locate the source.

And then he spots his truck sitting in the middle of the junkyard about a hundred yards away. The driver-side door is open. Slaughter trots in an anxious circle beside it.

Shane gets out of the car. He's relieved to see his dog and his truck again, but why does the truck appear abandoned? What happened to Dawn? Where are the Piranhaz?

He can figure out those mysteries once he's reclaimed his truck. He scrambles to the chain link fence, starts to climb.

Slaughter spots him, lets out a happy *yelp*, runs toward the fence, tail wagging.

"*Nagaashkaa*" Shane calls out – Ojibway for stop. Slaughter pulls up.

RAINBOW

Stomps down the street alongside a sprawling junkyard. She massages her injured shoulder. It itches where Bones stitched her up, but if she touches the actual wound, she gets a blinding stab of pain. Somewhere a stray dog barks incessantly, the sharp sound ricocheting through her aching head. Everything has gone to hell since that fucking trucker fought them off on the road to Mt. Tucker. When she finally gets ahold of him, she is going to make sure his agony dwarfs hers.

Somewhere in the distance, someone yells something she can't make out. The dog stops barking. Maybe it wasn't a stray after all. That trucker had a dog. Rainbow scans the street for the source of the voice.

A teenage boy bolts out of an alley a block ahead. He arcs straight toward Rainbow, but he's looking back over his shoulder at the alley as if fearful of what might come out after him.

The kid runs half a block before he finally turns his gaze forward and sees Rainbow. He stumbles to a stop fifty feet away.

It's the kid who was in the truck with the girl. Rainbow allows herself a slight smile. Maybe something is finally going to go her way today.

"Come 'ere kid!" She yells.

The boy panics, bolts the other direction–

Rainbow unleashes a volley from her AR-5 over his head. The boy collapses to the ground, weeping.

SHANE

Freezes at the sound of gunfire, straddling the top of the fence. From this vantage point, he can see the rainbow-mohawked woman on the street on the far side of the junkyard walking toward a cowering teenage boy.

Shane drops back to the ground outside of the fence. Slaughter *yelps* quizzically. But Shane doesn't want to draw the gangster's attention by yelling out commands.

So, he runs back to the Caddy, grabs the CB handset. "Slaughter, *kego*"

Slaughter hears Shane through the truck CB. Jumps into the cab.

"*Biidoon* Slaughter," Shane commands over the CB. "*Biidoon.*"

A moment later, Slaughter emerges from the truck cab dragging Shane's duffle bag full of money.

RAINBOW

Yanks the teenage boy to his feet. He's soft, delicate… pathetic.

"Please don't hurt me!" the kid begs through tears. "Please!"

"Tell me where the truck is," Rainbow growls.

He points into the junkyard. "It's right over there. It got a flat tire."

Rainbow follows his finger. She can just see the truck's bright red wind deflector over the piles of rubbish and scrap, about fifty yards away. She grins.

Rainbow releases the boy and pulls out a walkie-talkie.

BONES

Paces. Tyler has the girl pinned against the interior door of the repair depot. She's clearly frightened out of her mind, but she's doing her best not to show it. The other Piranhaz have arrayed themselves in a half circle to enjoy the show.

"I'm getting tired of asking," Bones snarls.

The girl juts out her chin. "Then why don't you stop?"

"Just tell us where the truck is, and we'll let you go."

"Yeah, right. If you hurt me, you'll pay for it."

Bones laughs. "Who's going to make me pay? That chickenshit little boyfriend of yours? That trucker?"

Rainbow's voice crackles over Bones' walkie-talkie, "Bones, where are you?"

He toggles the radio. "Where am I? Where the hell are you?"

"About fifty yards from the truck."

"Is that so." He turns to the girl with a sad smile. "You should've talked when it was worth something."

RAINBOW

Depresses the button on her walkie talkie. "It's in a junkyard just outside the rail yard."

She notices the boy inching away from her.

He notices her notice and makes his break – darts for the nearest building, a squat warehouse.

The little prick is getting on her last nerve. She toggles the walkie talkie. "Do we need the boy for anything?"

"Not really," Bones replies.

"Good."

The boy reaches the warehouse – but the door is locked. He tugs on the handle desperately, as if he can snap the bolt with his skinny arms. Rainbow mows him down with a burst from her assault rifle.

The impact throws him against the door. He pushes himself back, leaving a splatter of blood on the door. He wobbles a few steps up the sidewalk before falling into a pile of trash bags stacked against the wall of the warehouse.

Rainbow heads back up the street toward the truck.

Bones and the other Piranhaz find Rainbow lounging by a gaping hole where something big tore through the junkyard fence. She's looking mighty smug.

"This way," she says and leads them through the gap.

Bones follows, Tyler pushing the girl along beside him. The other Piranhaz fan out, keeping a wary eye. The trucker is still out there somewhere.

The truck sits a few dozen yards beyond the fence, mostly hidden by mounds of junk. The front tire is flat.

It's been a long couple of days to get this loot, but if the trucker has as much money as Rainbow said, it'll be worth it.

Rainbow jumps inside the cab. Pulls up a flap of carpet under the passenger seat, revealing a hatch to a secret compartment. She opens the hatch.

And screams in frustration. "It's gone! The money's gone!"

Bones climbs in and stares into the empty cavity. His jaw tightens.

SHANE

Watches the gangsters search his truck from the north side of the junkyard, leaning against Preacher's Lyriq. Slaughter sits next to him, the duffle bag of money hanging from his mouth.

The gangsters have Dawn. She appears unharmed. The rainbow-mohawked gangster killed Dawn's boyfriend, but it didn't look like Dawn saw the body where it fell in the pile of trash. Shane's heart aches. The girl's going to be devastated when she finds out.

Assuming he can rescue her before she ends up like the boy.

Shane reaches into the car and retrieves the CB handset. "Find what you were looking for?"

BONES

Stares at the CB. So, super trucker is watching them. That means he's nearby… with the money.

Rainbow grabs the handset. "Listen you mother–"

Bones snatches it from her. Takes a deep breath. Threats are not going to get them what they want, but they do have some leverage. Bones presses the button on the handset. "Nice trick. What's your name, by the way?"

From the CB: "My call sign's Kodiak. Who are you?"

"Everyone calls me Bones. My associate, the one you shot in the shoulder, is Rainbow. All right, Kodiak, here's the deal. We have the girl. We'll trade her to you for the money. All the money. Don't try to get cute."

SHANE

Doesn't like the sound of that. He needs to stall, figure out a plan. "What makes you think I care about the girl?"

"I'm willing to bet you're too much of a hero for your own good," Bones replies over the CB. "And if I'm wrong, well, we can always sell her to cover our gas money on this little adventure."

"I've already left the area," Shane says. "I can meet you later today." Bones will probably know that's a lie, but maybe it'll buy Shane some time.

There's a pause before Bones replies. "We're heading back to Ashford today. Bring the money to the intersection of Hesby and Berendo at midnight tonight, and you get the girl and your truck. And don't be stupid. Come alone."

Midnight. That gives him a little over twelve hours. It'll take at least seven to get to Ashford. Not much wiggle room. He toggles the handset. "I want her unspoiled, Bones."

"Then don't be late."

Chapter 14

Shane fingers the handle of his coffee mug. La Llorona sits opposite him in the booth in the Good Eats Diner, mouth agape as he concludes his story.

"...so, basically, the exchange is supposed to happen in about two hours."

"Wow."

"Yeah."

La Llorona runs a hand through her ink-black hair. "Shane, you can't give them your money. I mean, I feel for the girl, but her father won't be able to pay you back. You're not a superhero; you're a truck driver."

"Who doesn't currently have a truck."

"You can get a new truck. You can work security for convoys in the meantime. Call the police and walk away."

Shane raises an eyebrow. "You think the police will save her?"

La Llorona sighs. "Okay, yes, the world sucks now. And yes, the cops are not much use in the plague zones. But that's not your fault. This is not your responsibility."

Shane considers her point. This is certainly not what he expected when he took this job. It would be easy to walk away, tell Joe Harding that gangsters got his daughter before Shane could bring her back. Of course, the Piranhaz took Dawn as leverage against Shane, so in a way he was the one who got her into her current predicament. But the plague zones are dangerous for everyone. If it wasn't the Piranhaz, someone else probably would have gotten to Dawn. Walking away was the smart move, the survival move. Still, his decision really comes down to one thing.

"I can't leave her to those scum, L."

La Llorona leans back and studies him. "Well, well, well. Look who turns out to be an old softy."

Shane signals Kim for a refill of his coffee. It's gone cold. "I need you to do me a favor, L."

A gibbous moon dances among wispy clouds as Shane saunters up the middle of a two-lane street in a deserted section of Ashford that was zoned for commercial use back when anybody cared about zoning. He's put on a long duster and carries the black duffle bag in his left hand. The few working streetlights cast eerie circles of yellow among the blues and blacks. Trash blows by like tumbleweeds.

It's showdown time.

Shane shivers despite the duster. He has a plan. It's a good one, too, although there are a lot of moving parts. In Shane's experience, the more complex the plan, the less it's worth once bullets start flying. But having a plan is better than not having one.

Shane stops in the middle of the intersection of Hesby and Berendo. Checks his phone. Two minutes to twelve.

He waits.

The *rumble* of gas engines cuts through the wind. A few moments later, four motorcycles round a corner three blocks away. They drive forward, coming to a stop fifty feet from Shane, spread out across the roadway. Shane's back tenses. Where's Bones? Where's Dawn? Is this some kind of double-cross?

One of the cyclists pulls out a walkie-talkie. "He's here."

Shane's truck appears like a phantom from around the corner, its electric engine inaudible under the grumbling motorcycles. Dawn is tied spread eagle across the front, bound to the bars of the grill protector She's covered in dust and grit but appears uninjured.

Four cars round the corner and flank the truck, two on either side. The five vehicles pull into line with the motorcycles. Shane grimaces in the harsh assault of their headlights, all focused on him, as the bikers *rev* their engines threateningly.

Talk about outnumbered.

Shane meets Dawn's eyes. Tears stream down her cheeks, washing trails in the grime.

"They hurt you?" he shouts.

Dawn shakes her head.

A gangster with bones tattooed on his bald head and arms gets out of the driver's side of the truck. Must be the one called Bones. The rainbow-mohawked gangster – the one called Rainbow – gets out of the passenger side. Their nicknames are kind of literal, but it makes them easier to identify, and nobody said gangsters were clever.

"She's fine," Bones says. "I'm a man of my word."

Shane gives him a skeptical look.

"Hey, you think I like how things turned out?" Bones asks. "You think I like tormenting people? This is the world we live in now. Before the pandemic hit, I was going to be a doctor."

Rainbow looks at him, surprised. "I thought they kicked you out of medical school for stealing opioids."

Bones shoots her an angry look. "Not the point, Rainbow."

"Sorry."

Bones turns back to Shane. "Enough talk. You bring the money?"

Shane opens the duffle bag, revealing stacks of bills.

DAWN

Feels a flood of relief seeing the bag of money. She was sure Shane wouldn't show. Why would he? She's given him nothing but trouble. The gangsters taunted her on the drive up from Renton, but they didn't hurt her. It was no picnic being tied to the front of the truck for the last few blocks – she was able to position her feet on the bumper to support most of her weight, but the ropes dig into her wrists, and her shoulders and arms are starting to ache. If Shane didn't show, though… she heard enough from these gangsters to imagine what they would do to her then. She shudders thinking about it.

But Shane is here, and he brought the money. It'll be over soon.

"Toss it on the ground," Bones orders.

Shane tosses the bag out in front of him.

Bones motions to the motorcyclists to retrieve it. As they start forward, Bones leans in to Rainbow, whispers, "When they verify it's all there, you can kill him."

Dawn goes cold. "Shane," she yells, "it's a trap!"

SHANE

Smiles at Dawn's warning. It's a nice gesture, but he's way ahead of her.

When the bikers are about halfway to him, he reaches into the pockets of the duster and brings out two handfuls of caltrops – pairs of four-inch nails twisted and welded together like jacks. Any way they land, a spike points up. La Llorona loaned them to him from a homemade defense mechanism she installed on her rig.

He tosses the caltrops in a wide arc in front of him. The motorcycles hit the spikes – tires *blow* – the bikes swerve, hit each other, go down in a pile of metal and flesh.

And in a flash Shane dives to the ground, rolls behind the twisted mess of bikes and bikers.

Bones' face contorts with rage. "Kill him!"

Several of the Piranhaz open fire. Shane flattens against the pavement as the bullets finish off the wounded bikers he's using for cover.

So far, so good. Shane is positioned right where he wanted to be – next to the manhole cover in the center of the intersection. He pulls a short gaff hook from the duster's big inner pocket, the kind of hook with a perpendicular wooden handle. He loops the hook in the slot in the manhole cover. Yanks the iron cover up, slides it to the side. The thing weighs a ton.

He slithers into the manhole.

BONES

Motions for the two end cars – the yellow Volkswagen ID.4 and the grey Tesla Model 3 with its railroad spikes and missing side panel – to move forward. The cars screech around the pile of motorcycles and bodies to the manhole. Several Piranhaz hop out and approach the black opening.

SHANE

Climbs to his feet in knee-deep sludge. Almost pukes from the putrid stench. Instead, he retrieves a hand grenade from an inner pocket, pulls the pin. Drops it in the muck and hauls ass down the sewer.

BONES

Watches his men approach the manhole carefully.... they peer in, guns ready....

KA-BOOM!

An explosion sends flames and sewage out through the manhole. Two Piranhaz are blown back – hit the pavement, down for the count.

Bones strides forward. His head throbs with rage. How much more is he going to sacrifice for this money? He grabs the duffle bag, ignoring the splatter of smoldering fecal matter on it. Pulls out a stack of bills. Rifles it. Only the top one is real. The rest is cut paper.

The rage threatens to overwhelm him. His vision tunnels. He forces it back. Now is not the time to lose control.

He edges up to the manhole. "Kodiak, you have ten seconds to come out of there or the girl dies."

He motions to Rainbow. She steps up beside Dawn. Puts her hunting knife to the girl's throat.

SHANE

Stumbles down the sewer using the flashlight on his phone to guide his way. The beam finds the ladder up to the next manhole. He climbs up. Slides the cover open as quietly as he can. Now that the motorcycles are down, it's harder to be stealthy. He pokes his head out of the manhole.

He's a block away, behind and to the left of the Piranhaz. He can see Rainbow holding a wicked looking knife to Dawn's neck. This is the riskiest part of his plan. He didn't know how long he'd have before Bones decided to off Dawn.

Bones begins to count, "Ten… nine…"

Shane climbs out onto the street. He crouch-runs through the shadows toward the gangsters. Hopefully they don't smell him coming.

"Eight…" Bones continues, "Seven…"

Shane hunches to stay below windows and rearview mirrors as he scampers up behind the car to the left of his truck, a pale green Prius. The back window is open. Shane pulls the pin on another grenade, tosses it in.

"Six… Five…"

Shane crosses behind the truck.

"Four… Three…"

Shane creeps up between the truck and the Jeep Cherokee to its right. Rainbow is just ahead. Shane finds one more caltrop in his pocket. Shoves it under the back of the Cherokee's rear wheel.

"Two..."

Rainbow presses the knife blade against the soft, pale skin of Dawn's throat–

"One…"

KA-BOOM!!!!

The Prius explodes in a fiery ball. The concussion wave launches a shower of glass and steel across the intersection.

Everyone cringes – including Rainbow.

Well, not everyone. Not Shane. He was waiting to use the distraction to his advantage.

He leaps forward – pistol-whips Rainbow. She collapses to the asphalt – out cold. The knife clatters from her hand.

Shane hops in his truck and slides into the driver's seat. The key fob is resting in the center console. A lucky break. He throws the truck in reverse – peels out, tires *SQUEALING.*

The remaining Piranhaz regain their senses, open fire – but Shane's now barreling up the street, away from trouble.

DAWN

Clutches the bars of the truck's grill guard. She's grateful to have the knife away from her throat, but her current situation is only marginally better. The wind whips at her. Her shoulders throb at the strain.

She cranes her head to look back over the hood of the truck. The Jeep Cherokee backs out of the row of Piranhaz vehicles to pursue – but its rear tire hits something and blows.

Bones hops in the grey Tesla and hits the gas, falling in behind the truck. The Volkswagen ID.4 follows.

SHANE

Can't go too fast with Dawn lashed to his grill guard. The Tesla and VW are closing the gap quickly.

Shane rounds a corner – the Piranhaz right behind–

And there waiting for them are half a dozen big rigs. La Llorona and Sheik are behind the wheels of the front two.

Shane's shoulders sag in relief. He wasn't sure if La Llorona would be able to convince the others.

But his friends are there for him.

BONES

Skids the Tesla to a halt, leaving long streaks of rubber on the asphalt, as super trucker flies between the two leading big rigs. The VW swerves – narrowly avoids rear-ending Bones.

Fury threatens to overwhelm Bones, but he fights it down. Super trucker just took out half a dozen

Piranhaz all by himself. Now that he has backup, Bones doesn't like the odds. There'll be another time and another place.

Bones spins around, takes off. The VW follows.

The truckers hit their horns in celebration.

SHANE

Pulls his truck to a stop in the midst of the other rigs.

He jumps out, cuts Dawn free. She falls into his arms, weeping.

"Are you okay?" he asks.

"I want to go home."

Chapter 15

La Llorona opens the door to her truck and Slaughter leaps out, barking happily. Shane bends down to give him a good head rub, accepting his wet canine kisses.

"Okay, Slaughter, *kego*. *Kego*." Shane stands and gives La Llorona a fist bump. "Thanks, L. I owe you big time."

La Llorona smiles and shakes her head, her dangling pentagram earrings tinkling. "Don't worry about it, Kodiak. She seems like a nice kid. You did good."

"Thanks." Shane feels a hundred pounds lighter. And exhausted. He could sleep for a month.

"But," La Llorona adds, "when you get a chance, you could help me make more caltrops to replace the ones I gave you."

Shane smiles. "Deal."

Shane turns back to his truck. Dawn is crouched down by the open door, petting Slaughter. She's finally smiling, but it's a weary smile. Slaughter jumps up on her, almost knocking her over.

"Slaughter, *gawishmo*," Shane says.

But Dawn laughs as Slaughter licks at her neck and chin. "I'm glad to see you again, too, Slaughter. Come on, back in the truck now." She gestures toward the open door, and Slaughter hops up into the cab. Dawn starts to follow.

"Dawn," Shane says, stopping her. He's been dreading this moment. "There's something I need to tell you. About Eric."

Dawn's shoulders slump. "I guess everyone was right about him. I really thought he was special. But he ditched me when things got tough. I loved him so much, and he just abandoned me to those thugs."

There's no way to make this easier, so he just says it. "Eric's dead."

Dawn blanches. "What?"

"Rainbow killed him. I saw it happen. I'm sorry."

Dawn looks at the ground for a long moment. Sniffles. When she looks up, there are tears in her eyes. "I don't know how to feel."

"You can feel awful. Because it's awful. No matter what he did, he didn't deserve that."

And now her tears start flowing. Shane steps up, pulls her into a hug.

"Man, love sucks," Dawn sobs into his shoulder.

"You got that right."

The sun is peeking above the tree line when Shane pulls off on the side of the highway to Mt. Tucker.

Dawn sits in the passenger seat, legs curled under her, petting Slaughter absently. Slaughter's tail thumps a regular beat against the floor.

"You ready?" Shane asks.

"I guess so. You've got to get paid, right?"

Shane studies her. She's staring out the side window into the woods, her mouth set in a tight line.

"Dawn... if you don't want to go back, I'm not going to make you."

She sighs. "What else can I do? Looks like I'm doomed to spend the rest of my life in Mount Tucker. But I'm telling you, no way am I marrying Steve Englehoff."

"Hey," Shane says, "regardless of what happened with Eric, you held your own out here. I'm impressed."

"Thanks."

Slaughter huffs, nudges Dawn's leg. She gives him a vigorous scratch behind the ears. "Guess this is goodbye, boy."

Dawn climbs up into the back of the truck's trailer after Shane. They stopped at the Good Eats Diner as soon as it opened to retrieve the trailer from storage. Then they went to a twenty-four-hour thrift store to buy the old, green trunk that currently sits against the trailer's back wall, lonely in the echoey space.

Shane opens the lid of the trunk and spreads a blanket across the bottom. "I called your dad. He'll be waiting at the loading dock."

Dawn nods. She steps into the trunk and curls up on the blanket. It's surprisingly roomy.

Shane hands her a pillow. "I need to seal the trunk, but it's not airtight. Just stay relaxed and try not to move too much."

Dawn adjusts the pillow under her head. "I'll be fine as long as they keep it right side up."

Shane nods. "Well. It's been nice knowing you."

Dawn extends a hand. "Thank you. I know I didn't want your help at first, but I'm really glad you came after me."

Shane shakes her hand. "Me too."

"And we can keep in touch. Text me any time."

Shane nods and closes the lid.

Dawn smiles. If they're going to communicate after she's back in Mt. Tucker, she'll probably have to be the one to reach out.

Dawn hears the trunk's latches *click* shut, then the sound of tape coming off a roll. It's official clean zone tape, used to seal packages for transport through the plague zones to ensure the contents aren't contaminated. Shane shouldn't have it, but you'd have to be pretty naïve to think there weren't plenty of rolls floating around outside the clean zones.

It's not pitch black in the trunk. A bit of light seeps in around the seams. A tickle of panic wells up in Dawn's chest, but she takes a deep breath and fights it back down. She's certain she could force the lid of the trunk open if she had to. Thank goodness she's not claustrophobic.

Shane's footsteps recede, then there's a *bang-bang* – the rear doors of the truck trailer closing.

Now it *is* pitch black in the trunk. In a way, that makes it easier. Dawn tries to doze for the short drive the rest of the way to Mt. Tucker. She isn't successful.

Less than fifteen minutes later, the truck comes to a stop. A few minutes after that, the back doors of the trailer open and light once again seeps into the trunk. There is a pause of several more minutes. The panic starts to intrude again. Dawn tries to think of something good. Her first thought is of Eric, but that image no longer brings pleasant feelings. She thinks of Slaughter. Maybe she should ask her parents for a dog again.

Yeah, right. She's going to be grounded until she's twenty-five.

Footsteps approach. Two people, it sounds like. They lift the trunk. Dawn presses her hands and feet against the sides to keep from shifting. This is the dangerous part of the plan. If they discover her in here, she'll be banned from Mt. Tucker forever.

The people carry her into the loading dock.

Someone says, "Sign here."

And then she hears her father's voice. "Give this to Mr. Carpenter."

Dawn didn't realize how much she missed her parents, but she feels a pang of sadness as well. After everything she went through, she's going to end up right back where she started. Stuck.

Her parents carry the trunk outside. They aren't as steady with it as the people from the loading dock. She hears their car's back hatch close and then the front doors open and close.

"Dawn?" her mother says. "Are you okay?"

"Yes."

A sob. And then her father: "We can't let you out until we're inside the house. Someone might see."

"I understand."

Ten more minutes and the trunk is sitting in the middle of the living room. Dawn hears the tape peeled off. The latches click open.

And then the lid rises. She blinks, though the light is dim – all the curtains are closed.

Her parents are standing over her. Her mom weeps, chest heaving. A few tears run down her dad's cheeks, too. She can't remember ever seeing him cry before.

He reaches down for her with both hands, lifts her out of the trunk.

The three of them embrace in the middle of the dim living room.

For better or worse, she's home.

The clerk slides a package the size of a loaf of bread across the counter to Shane. It's wrapped in brown paper and an unusually large amount of duct tape. "From Joe Harding."

Shane resists the temptation to rip it open right there on the loading dock. He has to stay cool, not arouse suspicion. He orders a meal from Claire's – pot roast and a piece of cherry pie. Then he tosses the package nonchalantly in the truck cab and takes Slaughter for a walk.

Only after Slaughter's done his business does Shane climb into the truck cab, retrieve the package, and move back into the sleeping area. He cuts through the duct tape, rips back the paper. Inside are stacks of cash, a mix of twenties and hundreds, bound with rubber bands.

He considers the money for a few moments. It's possibly the biggest payday he's ever had, but he doesn't feel much like celebrating. He shrugs, counts it. Twenty-five thousand, as promised. He adds it to the cash in the secret compartment under the passenger seat.

He calls Little Zeke. "It's Shane. I've got it all... Two days. Maybe three."

Dawn enters the Mt. Tucker Baskin Robbins. The tinkling bell above the door, the pastel decor, the sparkling cleanliness, and the chilled air are all comfortably familiar. Her father thought it would be good for her to be seen around town as soon as possible to alleviate any suspicion. So, she put on her small-town-girl clothes – jeans, cute blue top that brings out her eyes, milk-chocolate-brown ankle boots – and went out for ice cream.

Three of her girlfriends are pecking at single scoops of low-fat frozen yogurt at a table in the corner. They're her age but seem younger. Pretty. Thin. Airheads.

As she approaches, they stare at her wide-eyed. "What did you do to your hair?" Hannah gasps.

Dawn runs her hand through her short, black locks. She'd almost forgotten about that. “I'm just trying something.”

“It looks kind of... weird,” Ashley says. “Where have you been, anyway?”

“I wasn't feeling well.”

The girls all pull back instinctively, horror in their eyes.

“It was a migraine,” Dawn adds quickly. “I'm fine now.”

“You're sure?” Hannah asks.

“I'm sure.”

“You missed Jane's party,” Margie says with a sly smile. “Steve was talking to Riley all night.”

Dawn rolls her eyes. “I don't care.”

“Sure you don't,” Ashley says, and the girls giggle.

Dawn sighs and sits down. These are her friends. What else is she going to do?

Shane drives away from Mt. Tucker, through the foothills. Slaughter dozes in back. The truck cab seems oddly quiet. Nothing unusual, but for the first time in he-can’t-remember-how-long it bothers him. He turns up the radio.

The road takes a gentle turn, then stretches out ahead in a long straightaway. A group of three cars and two motorcycles are coming toward him in the distance. Shane’s hands tighten on the wheel. One of the cars is an unfamiliar black Camry with a machine gun mounted on the hood. But the others are not unfamiliar: a yellow Volkswagen ID.4 hatchback and a grey Tesla bristling with iron spikes and missing a side panel.

It's the Piranhaz.

Shane hits the brakes. Makes a three-point U-turn as he grabs the CB handset. “Breaker two-four for Mt. Tucker, come back.”

The voice of a town guardsman responds, “This is Mt. Tucker, go ahead.”

“This is Kodiak. I'm heading back, and I need help. Lots of help. Over.”

“Copy that. We've got your back. Over.”

Shane floors it, keeping one eye on his mirrors. The Piranhaz are closing, but he should be able to reach cover from the guard tower before they catch him.

He rounds a bend. Mt. Tucker comes into view in the distance, the guard tower rising against the blue sky. He’s going to make it.

Then – something’s moving on an overgrown farm road to the right of town. Shane squints…

It’s a flatbed tow truck – with a WWII era *Sherman tank* chained on its bed. The tank is trackless and rusty. The white star on the turret has a Piranhaz symbol spray-painted over it in red.

Shane’s heart sinks.

RAINBOW

Sticks her head out through the hatch on the tank's turret. The side of her face is swollen, both eyes ringed with purple bruising. But the pain is drowned out by the fury coursing through her. She can see the back of Carlos's shaved head at the wheel of the truck, his cheesy, peacock-feather earring bouncing to the ruts and bumps of the dirt road.

As Mt. Tucker comes into view, Rainbow ducks in and closes the hatch.

She sits at the gun and turret controls. That part of the tank works fine. Tyler assists her, a pile of shells at his feet. Rainbow sights through the scope – gets the guard tower in her crosshairs.

Squeezes the trigger.

The tank's big gun fires, the vehicle vibrating with the deep *BOOM*. The shell arcs through the air, into the guard tower–

KABLAM – the guard tower explodes!

And collapses in a pile of debris, a shower of kindling drifting down across the entry gate and road.

Rainbow grins.

Dawn leaps to her feet as a blast rattles the windows of the Baskin Robbins.

"What was that?" Hannah cries.

"Come on!" Dawn shouts. She bolts for the door.

The others follow.

They run out onto Main Street. There's a smoldering pile of rubble where the guard tower once stood. Townspeople come running from all directions to see what's going on.

Dawn has a sneaking suspicion she knows.

Rainbow pushes the handle to turn the tank's turret to the left. Tyler is reloading the big gun – it's clearly not a process with which he's experienced.

The abandoned fruit stand comes into Rainbow's sights. She sweeps the gun along the road.

And the red truck with the bear claw symbol comes into view.

"Got him!" Rainbow tracks the truck with the turret.

"Make sure you lead him," Tyler says.

"I know! Just tell me when you're ready." Rainbow sets the crosshairs a dozen yards ahead of the truck, keeps tracking...

Tyler gets the next shell in place. "Fire away."

Rainbow hits the trigger – the tank shell rockets out, toward Shane's truck–

Rainbow led a little too much. The shell passes in front of the truck – PLOWS into an old fuel tank by the fruit stand–

And out the other side – explodes in a field, throwing up a plume of dirt and grass.

Rainbow pumps her fist. "Just missed. Reload!"

SHANE

Hits the brakes.

Oil spills out of the ruptured fuel tank – oozes across the roadway–

Shane's truck hits the oil – he takes his foot off the brake, but it's no use – the truck skids–

Slides off the road – down a slope – through a wire fence–

CRUNCHES into a rusted-out tractor in the ditch next to the dirt farm road that parallels the highway here.

Shane presses down on the accelerator, but the tractor is wedged between the truck and the edge of the ditch. The truck can't push through it.

So, Shane throws the truck into reverse. The tires spin in the oily mud. He can't get traction.

He grabs the CB. "Bones!"

Bones' voice crackles back, "Hello, Kodiak. Not so cocky now, are you?"

"Bones, if you blow me up, you'll blow up the money, too."

"I no longer care about the money."

Shane has no reply for that. He looks out at the tank on the flatbed – and into the big 75mm gun aimed straight at him.

Chapter 16

Dawn and her friends run to the main gate. A couple dozen other townspeople are already arrayed along the chain link fence watching the action. Dawn spots the mayor, fingers laced in the links. More people join the growing crowd every second. Dawn's parents jog down Main Street toward her.

Beyond the fence, Shane's truck is angled down the slope between the main road and the dirt farm road that parallels it on the left. The truck appears to be wedged against the old tractor that's been slowly rusting in the ditch ever since Mr. Welker went bankrupt.

A flatbed tow truck with an army tank lashed on its bed rumbles along the other farm road, the one that runs perpendicular to the main road. Up on the main road, a group of familiar Piranhaz vehicles approach.

From what Dawn can see, Shane is screwed.

She turns to the others. "We've got to do something! We've got to help him!"

Hannah looks at her like she's crazy. "We can't leave quarantine."

"Who cares about quarantine! They're going to kill him."

"Dawn, the rules are clear," the mayor says gently. "Nobody can go in or out. For any reason."

Is her town really so selfish? Maybe if she tries another tack. "When they get done with him, what do you think they're going to do to us?"

"The militia's already mustering," the mayor says. "Those thugs won't get past this gate."

Dawn gestures toward Shane. "But that won't help him!"

Her dad puts his arm around her shoulders. "It's unfortunate, Sweetie, but since that gang took out the watchtower, there's not much we can do. I'm afraid Mr. Carpenter is going to have to get out of this himself."

Dawn shrugs him off. "I can't believe this! After what he did for me?"

Her dad blanches. "Dawn, shh!"

"You're all monsters!" She pushes through the crowd, runs back into town. If they won't help, she'll have to figure something out herself.

RAINBOW

Wipes sweat from her forehead. She looks down at Tyler, who's struggling with the spent shell. "What's taking so long?"

"It's jammed!"

Rainbow checks on the truck through the gun sights, takes a deep breath to calm down, coughs on the acrid, humid air in the tank. There's time. The truck is still wedged against the tractor, its wheels kicking up mud in a fruitless attempt to back up the oily slope. The trucker could get out and run, but the quarantine town would never let him past its gate, and there's nowhere else for him to hide.

She can afford to be patient.

She can afford to savor the moment.

DAWN

Runs to city hall, a brick building with roman columns a block up Main Street. She circles around back to where the town vehicles are kept. The dark green Ford F-150 Lightning is still parked where she saw them attaching the yellow snowplow a week ago in anticipation of possible early storms.

The pickup truck's door is unlocked. The key fob under the visor. In a small town like this, nobody worries much about theft, especially since the fence went up.

Dawn drives the pickup back around to Main Street. Once she's got a straight shot to the gate, she pushes the accelerator to the floor.

Members of the town militia are gathering to one side of the gate. A few of the spectators are retreating to hide, but most are still frozen in place, watching the drama unfold beyond the fence.

Dawn lays on the horn.

The townspeople look back, then scramble out of the way when they see the snowplow barreling towards them.

Dawn braces herself – *KA-BANG* – the plow crashes through the gate.

She careens off the main highway, bouncing down the slope and onto the old farm road, the truck fishtailing in the dirt. She heads for Shane and the rusted-out tractor, kicking up clouds of dust.

RAINBOW

Spots the snowplow in the gun sights. Is the town actually risking its clean zone status to help the trucker? She pounds a fist against the inside of the turret. "Tyler!"

With a last, mighty heave, Tyler pries the spent shell free. "Got it!

He grabs a new shell, loads it. Rainbow centers Kodiak's truck in the sights.

SHANE

Stares dumbfounded at the pickup bouncing toward him. Is that Dawn behind the wheel? The girl must have a death wish.

The pickup swerves into the ditch and slams into the rusty tractor with a thunderous metallic *CRUNCH*. The plow attachment sends the tractor tumbling. The pickup bounces back up onto the farm road and keeps moving.

Free of the blockage, the truck slides down into the shallow ditch–

Shane puts pedal to metal. The truck's tires catch traction in the dirt–

BOOM – a shell arcs from the tank's gun–

Shane punches the accelerator – the truck lurches forward, up out of the ditch – Shane cranks the wheel, turns the truck onto the farm road–

KABLAM – the shell slams into the slope Shane just vacated. The explosion rocks the truck trailer as he pulls away, briefly lifting the wheels on one side off the ground.

But they settle back onto the road, and Shane shifts into high gear.

RAINBOW

Pounds on the gun with both fists. “Damn it! Damn it! Reload!”

DAWN

Steers the pickup truck down the dirt farm road parallel to the paved highway where the other group of Piranhaz – the cars and motorcycles – races toward her.

They open fire as she passes – handguns, shotguns, mounted machine gun – a cacophony of *BANGS, BLAMS, RAT-A-TAT-TATS.*

The pickup isn't bullet proof. Dawn *screams* – ducks – as bullets perforate the truck's body, shatter the windows, *ping* off the plow.

But none hit her.

She flies past the Piranhaz.

SHANE

Scowls at the assault on poor Dawn. He’s a hundred yards behind her. He veers right – across the shallow ditch, through the low fence, up the slope, onto the highway – his truck lurches dangerously–

He flies into the cluster of Piranhaz vehicles – *SMASHES* into the side of the black Camry–

The other Piranhaz scatter off the road as the crumpled Camry tumbles into the overgrown field.

The truck's trailer sways. Shane's stomach drops. He hits the accelerator to straighten the rig. The right-side wheels go off the pavement, kicking up gravel. But the trailer steadies. He guns the engine, back into the center of the asphalt, heading away from town.

DAWN

Finds an access point from the farm road to the highway. Turns onto it, barely slowing, the pickup skidding, leaving black streaks on the asphalt. Shane's big rig drops in behind her.

There's a CB radio mounted under the pickup's dash. She tunes it to channel twenty-four. "Shane?"

Shane's voice comes over the CB: "Dawn, are you okay?"

"I think so."

"Keep going – as fast as you can. Take the first exit you come to. I'll keep them away from you."

Dawn checks her side mirror. Behind the truck, the Piranhaz regroup, circle back, give chase.

Dawn pushes the accelerator to the floor.

RAINBOW

Tracks the big rig with the tank's gun sights as Tyler reloads. But the other Piranhaz are between them. Rainbow doesn't have a clean shot. The truck rounds a corner, disappears behind a hill.

Rainbow opens the hatch, pokes her head out.

Carlos, driving the flat bed, looks back at her.

"Follow them!" she screams.

Carlos nods and hits the accelerator.

The highway curves along the foothills – a gentle wooded drop on the right, a steep muddy slope up on the left. The Piranhaz have caught up to Shane – not too hard because he's not going that fast. He weaves back and forth, blocking the road, keeping them from getting past.

Up ahead, Dawn hauls ass in the snowplow, putting distance between her and the others. She approaches a turnoff – an old, paved road heading across a grassy plain. The snowplow careens onto it, fishtailing.

Good. Shane wants her safe while he deals with the Piranhaz.

RAINBOW

Scans the landscape through the tank gun sights. The flatbed/tank is on the highway now, a mile behind the action and slowly closing. Occasionally, Rainbow gets a glimpse of the big rig through the trees and hills, but she still hasn't gotten a clear shot. She turns the scope to scout the road ahead.

And spots the snowplow bouncing across the plain.

It's far from any cover.

Rainbow's mouth curls into an evil smile. Her mission is to end that fucking trucker's life today, but she can spare a shell to make his little sidekick pay for interfering.

Rainbow spins the big gun. Gets the snowplow in her sights.

Pulls the trigger.

DAWN

Tries to remember how she gets back to town from here. Mt. Tucker was already quarantined before she learned to drive.

KABOOM!

An explosion erupts a dozen yards from the snowplow.

The concussion rocks the pickup. Chunks of turf rain onto her windshield.

Dawn looks around desperately – spots the flatbed/tank on the highway behind and above her.

The cover of the woods is at least half a mile away. Dawn floors it.

RAINBOW

Pumps her fist. Almost got the meddling bitch.

Tyler reloads the big gun. He’s getting better at it.

Rainbow tracks the snowplow – leading it – getting the pace just right – not easy from a moving vehicle on a winding road.

She pulls the trigger – but as the shell fires, something crosses the gun sights–

The cab of the flatbed.

She's tracked the gun around to a forward facing and fired *through* the rear window of the cab.

The shell *CRASHES* out through the windshield of the flatbed – it's still on target–

Arcs through the air–

EXPLODES in the road a few feet in front of the snowplow.

SHANE'S

Stomach drops as the blast tosses the snowplow up – over–

It does a complete flip – lands wheels down – tumbles off the road – rolls through the tall grass – comes to a crumpled rest upside down.

RAINBOW

Throws open the tank hatch to see what she's done. The back window of the flatbed cab is gone – a few shards of glass hang from the frame. The windshield's gone too.

Oh, yeah, there's also empty space where Carlos's head should be.

But his hands are still on the wheel.

And the flatbed's still moving. Full speed.

And the road curves not too far ahead.

Rainbow leaps out of the hatch, scrambles across the front of the tank, dives through the rear window of the cab. She grabs the wheel with one hand, opens the driver's side door with the other. Shoves the headless body out and slides into its place. She jams the wheel left, fishtails around the corner – but she makes it. Regains control of the flatbed.

She growls angrily. Hits the accelerator.

DAWN

Spits. Her mouth tastes like pennies. But she's apparently still alive, hanging upside down from her seatbelt in the crushed snowplow cab.

She shakes the cobwebs from her head. Wipes blood from her nose.

She releases her seatbelt and falls painfully onto the crumpled roof of the ruined vehicle. Thank goodness the truck has a roll bar. Probably saved her life.

She drags herself through the shattered window. Climbs gingerly to her feet.

She can barely put weight on her right leg. Left shoulder's throbbing. Ache in her head like a shrieking baby. She's messed up… but not dead. She staggers toward the road.

SHANE

Lets out a long breath when he sees Dawn emerge from the snowplow. That crash would've killed a lot of people.

He checks his side mirror. He isn't the only one who's been watching Dawn's predicament. One of the Piranhaz motorcycles peels off and cuts overland toward the wreckage.

Shane punches the accelerator, races for the turnoff.

DAWN

Reaches the pavement just as she hears the motorcycle approaching. She freezes.

The biker opens fire with twin machine guns mounted on either side of his front fairing – bullets chew up the asphalt at Dawn's feet. She dives into the ditch beside the road. It's not much cover, but the stream of bullets passes over her.

SHANE

Careens onto the old road. He pushes the truck to its limits as he watches the motorcycle close on Dawn. The other Piranhaz are hot on his tail.

Shane flips up the cover over his special instruments. Triggers one of the switches–

A rocket streaks out of its cylinder–

Right on target.

KABOOM – the motorcycle is history.

Dawn crawls out of the ditch. Climbs to her feet.

Shane slows enough for her to hop onto the truck's running board, and then hits the accelerator before any of the Piranhaz can get up beside him. He opens the door and pulls Dawn inside. She tumbles over him, drags herself into the passenger seat, bloody and disheveled.

"You okay?" Shane asks.

"Relatively speaking."

He shakes his head. "That was brave what you did back there. I owe you one."

"I think we're past keeping score. What are we going to do about them?" She gestures at the side mirror.

Shane checks his own side mirror – the grey Tesla, yellow ID.4, and a motorcycle are close behind. Further back, the flatbed with its tank is catching up.

Shane’s jaw tightens. “I'm working on that.”

Chapter 17

The road winds back up into the hills. Rainbow pushes the flatbed at a dangerous pace. It lurches back and forth across the pavement on every curve. Her right calf aches from jamming the accelerator to the floor. The tank on back weighs a ton – thirty tons, actually. With that kind of load, the flatbed strains to keep up speed on the incline. But Rainbow doesn't give a shit if she burns out the engine.

She's closing on the cluster of Piranhaz vehicles, though her focus is on the cursed big rig farther ahead. She hits the horn. The Tesla and motorcycle swerve to one side of the road, the VW to the other, forming a lane. Rainbow flies through it.

The big rig is a hundred yards ahead, the gap narrowing. Rainbow wills the flatbed faster. Fifty yards… twenty-five… ten… five…

CRUNCH!

Rainbow plows straight into the back of the big rig's trailer.

SHANE

Fights the wheel as the trailer whipsaws across the road. Fortunately, the flatbed was only going about ten miles per hour faster than the big rig, and the protective rails welded on the trailer's back seem to have absorbed most of the impact. Still, it's all Shane can do to keep the truck from jackknifing. He hits the accelerator to pull the rig straight.

"What the hell?" Dawn cries, both hands braced against the dashboard.

Shane has no time to offer an opinion. He checks his side mirror.

The flatbed is approaching for another shot.

Shane pushes the truck faster. He's at the edge of control on this winding road, but he can't shake the flatbed and its deranged driver.

Then, ahead, a gravel turnout, about fifty feet long and fifteen feet wide, off to the right just before the road curves left. There's a sign at the center of the turnout, at the edge of the pavement – painted two-by-fours between two posts, welcoming drivers to the National Forest, a bear in a ranger hat warning about forest fires.

Shane veers right, into the turnout. Gravel sprays into the air.

"What are you doing?" Dawn cries, looking down. From her vantage point in the passenger seat, she'd be right above the steep, brush-covered slope at the far edge of the turnout.

Shane pulls back left, timing the move to impact the right side of the sign with his battering ram.

CRACK – the right post shatters – the sign spins, snapping the left post – the impact destroys the truck's left headlight, dents the side panel, but that's a small price to pay for what happens next.

The sign spins through the air, out over the road, the boards separating into dangerous projectiles.

RAINBOW

Is heading straight for the flying remains of the sign. She instinctively jams the wheel of the flatbed right – swerves into the gravel turnout.

The big rig pulls back onto the highway, tires squealing. It careens around the curve to the left, tilting dangerously from the g-forces.

The flatbed flies across the turnout, heading for the drop-off. Rainbow slams on the brakes – yanks the wheel hard left–

But the flatbed wasn't meant to handle like that, especially not with a heavy tank on its bed.

It tilts – goes over–

And rolls. Down the slope.

Rainbow clutches the wheel. Her head bangs against the ceiling, then she's thrown back down into the seat. Then it all happens again. Stars explode in her vision. Her wounded arm screams.

Somewhere in the chaos she looks into the mirror and sees a loose shell fly out of the open hatch of the tank turret.

And then the flatbed comes to a rest on its left side at the bottom of the slope.

Rainbow is crumpled in a pile inside the cab of the flat bed. She looks up blearily.

The shell is falling straight toward her.

Oh shit.

Rainbow tries to lunge through the shattered windshield as the shell falls through the window, into the cab–

KABOOM!

BONES

Winces at the ball of flame as Rainbow and the flatbed cab become confetti. Black smoke rises from the wreckage.

Rainbow was a wildcat, but she was also a loyal sidekick and great fun. Bones gives a salute in her memory.

He turns to Big O, the heavyset Latina with the shaved head driving the Tesla. "Rainbow had her shot. It's time to execute plan B."

Bones looks back over his shoulder to Malcolm and Lush in the back seat. "You ready?"

They nod.

Bones waves his arm out the window.

Maria, on the remaining motorcycle, pulls up beside him. Bones gives her a nod.

Maria nods back, peels away.

MARIA

Circles around on a rugged fire trail that leads up through the brush and trees and along the summit of the ridge of hills.

She catches up to the chase a couple miles later. Below her, the Tesla, bristling like a porcupine with its iron spikes, is tight on the big rig's tail, with the yellow

VW a dozen yards behind. The cars maintain their positions, keeping pressure on the truck and biding their time.

The hills are growing into mountains now, the fire trail and road cut into the sides of steeper, rocky slopes. Maria descends off the fire trail toward the others, bouncing down the rugged terrain, moving to intercept them where the main road carves through a shoulder of the ridge.

She pulls her crossbow from a holster on her saddlebags. It's loaded and ready.

As the truck moves into the pass cut through the purple-grey rock, Maria leaps the motorcycle off the higher slope–

Flies over the truck trailer–

Fires the crossbow downward–

The barbed bolt pierces the roof of the trailer, sticks. A twenty-foot cable attached to the back of the bolt uncoils from her saddle bag. Maria hits the far slope, her teeth rattling from the impact. The cable pulls free, trails out over the back of the truck's trailer, flapping down behind the big rig.

Maria bounces down the far slope, dodging brush and stubby trees, heading toward a road in the plains below.

It's up to the others now.

SHANE

Looks into the mirrors, trying to spot the source of the thump. It sounded like something hit the top of the truck, but he can't see anything out of the ordinary.

"What was that?" Dawn asks.

Shane shakes his head. “I don't know, but I don't think it was good.”

BONES

Turns to Malcolm and Lush. “Cable’s in place. You’re up.”

Malcolm and Lush climb out of the rear windows of the Tesla, using the spikes to pull themselves up onto the roof. From there, they make their way down onto the hood, stepping carefully between the spikes.

Big O edges the Tesla up close behind the truck.

Malcolm is short and stocky. He holds the taller Lush steady as Lush grabs for the swinging cable. After three tries, Lush gets his hands around it. Jumps off the car – swings to the truck trailer – landing with his feet against the rear doors. He uses the cable to climb hand-over-hand up onto the roof of the trailer.

He tosses the cable back to Malcolm.

SHANE

Can’t see what’s going on back on the rear of his trailer, but he has his suspicions. He opens the glove box and retrieves the new 9mm semi-automatic pistol he bought in Ashford to replace the one he lost. He slips it into the back of his waistband. “Take the wheel.”

“What?!” Dawn stares at him wide-eyed.

“I need to go do something.”

“Go? Go where?”

“I think we may have parasites. Take the wheel.”

Dawn obliges, sliding into the driver's seat as Shane opens the door and steps out onto the running board. He climbs up onto the hood of the truck, balancing on the swaying vehicle. Draws the pistol with one hand while steadying himself with the other against the windshield.

He peeks up over the cab's roof fairing. Two Pirahnaz are creeping toward him across the top of the trailer.

They spot him – go for their guns–

Shane fires – hits the tall gangster–

That one spins, falls off the back of the truck–

BONES

Cringes as Lush slams down onto the hood of the Tesla, impaled on three of the railroad spikes. Lush's mouth opens and closes, blood sputtering out.

If you want something done right, you gotta do it yourself.

Bones draws his SIG Sauer .45 automatic. Pulls himself out through the window.

Seated in the window, he motions to Mouse and Ken in the VW to move up. Then Bones climbs out onto the hood of the Tesla.

SHANE

Exchanges fire with the short gangster, who has dropped flat on the trailer.

Shane hits him between the eyes.

BONES

Makes his way across the hood of the Tesla, stepping over Lush's body. The truck blocks the wind here, but it's still precarious.

Bones lunges for the flapping cable. His fingers close around it. He swings over to the truck trailer. His boots slip on the rear doors, and for a moment he's swinging on the cable behind the truck. But he lifts his legs and gets his feet firmly planted.

He climbs hand-over-hand until he's just below the top of the trailer. Peeks up over the edge.

Malcolm lays unmoving on the roof of the trailer. At the opposite end of the trailer, the trucker peers over the cab's roof fairing.

Bones fires a spray of bullets across the trailer's roof.

SHANE

Ducks down as bullets *whiz* over his head. He meets Dawn's gaze through the windshield. She clearly thinks he's insane. Maybe she's right. His heart *thuds* in his chest.

The two-lane road splits, a pair of guardrails separating each lane. The second trailing car – the yellow Volkswagen ID.4 hatchback – pulls into the oncoming traffic lane, zooms up alongside the truck on the far side of the guardrail. A small, wiry gangster leans out the window with an HK416 assault rifle.

Panic wells in Shane's throat. He grabs the right-side mirror, slides down onto the running board on that side of the truck–

Just in the nick of time – the gangster opens fire – *CHUCK-A-CHUCK-A-CHUCK-A-CHUCK.*

Shane cowers as bullets *scream* overhead and *ping* off the truck's armor.

A pause in the barrage. Shane reaches up over the hood of the truck, returns fire, the *BANG-BANG* of the 9mm sounding anemic compared to the big assault rifle.

BONES

Needs to get creative. The trucker is expecting him to go over the roof of the trailer. So, Bones swings out to the right – and spots the trucker crouched on the running board, exchanging fire with Mouse in the VW.

Bones squeezes off a few shots.

SHANE

Presses himself against the cab as a bullet *pings* off the truck's side mirror. That one came from behind the truck. Shane spots Bones leaning around the back of the trailer. Shane returns fire – but Bones swings back out of sight.

On the other side of the truck, the VW speeds up.

DAWN

Clenches the wheel, eyes moving from the road to the VW on her left to Shane crouched outside the cab on her right. She varies her speed and swerves back and forth in the lane to make Shane a tougher target. The truck is harder to handle on the winding mountain road than on the freeway and straight surface streets of Renton.

Ahead, the guardrails end, the two lanes of the road rejoining.

The VW pulls into the right lane, in front of the truck. The back of the hatchback pops open. Inside, the short, wiry gangster crouches next to a metal canister full of black tar. He lights the tar with a lighter. Black smoke billows back over the truck.

SHANE
Coughs in the thick, acrid cloud.

Bones swings out from behind the trailer again, fires – Shane returns fire – but Bones swings back out of sight behind the truck.

DAWN
Is forced to slow down as the smoke from the VW obscures her vision. She squints into the dark, billowing haze. She can barely make out the front of the truck's nose.

No, wait… there's something moving in the smoke, ahead and to the right, vertical columns–

Trees!

The road is curving left – the truck's tires hit the gravel shoulder – Dawn *squeals* – jams the wheel hard left –

SHANE
Presses against the truck as he's whipped by tree branches.

BONES
Hanging from the cable, swings wildly, bouncing against the rear doors of the lurching trailer. He's thrown out to the right – branches pummel him – the gun flies from his hand.

SHANE

Sees Bones' pistol tumble off into the brush. Grins.

Then – *CRUNCH* – the trailer sideswipes a tree, sending shockwaves through the rig. Shane loses his footing on the running board, clings to the side mirror until he can regain his perch.

DAWN

Veers back onto the asphalt.

The road curves back and forth along the edge of the mountain. The truck moves in and out of the smoke – it still obscures Dawn's vision, but she can catch enough glimpses of terrain to stay on the pavement… and she doesn't dare stop.

Shane pulls himself up onto the hood of the cab. Gives her an encouraging nod.

BONES

Clings to the cable for dear life. He's feeling mighty naked without his gun. He climbs upward, hand-over-hand, lurches up onto the roof of the trailer. Malcolm's body is sprawled halfway up – his .22 revolver still clutched in his cold, dead hand–

The trucker stands up on the hood of the truck cab, pistol leveled at Bones.

He pulls the trigger–

CLICK!

Now it's Bones' turn to smile. The trucker is out of bullets.

Bones dives for Malcolm's revolver.

SHANE

Lunges up onto the cab roof, vaults over the fairing onto the trailer, bolts toward Bones–

Bones grabs the dead gangster's revolver – *BLAM*–

The shot takes a chunk out of the side of Shane's left biceps.

A spike of pain shoots through his arm. Stars pop in his vision.

But he keeps moving – leaps – right foot extended in a kick–

His boot connects with Bones' hand – the revolver tumbles off onto the road.

Shane hits the trailer, rolls past Bones, back up to his feet.

Bones lunges at Shane – fists flying.

Shane ducks, swings–

He and Bones exchange blows – circle like boxers – whipped by the smoky air rushing across the roof of the trailer. Shane is no lightweight – but Bones is the better fighter. Bones gets several good shots in – a body blow that echoes through Shane's ribs, a right hook that would've put Shane down if it didn't glance off his forearm. Arms up, Shane reminds himself, advice from a dozen movies.

Then – Bones connects with Shane's wounded biceps – pain shoots down Shane's arm, his stomach roils with nausea, the world spins. He staggers back – gets control in the nick of time. He's teetering near the back of the trailer.

Bones steps in to finish it – with a kick to Shane's chest–

Shane stumbles – off the truck–

But he reaches out with a flailing hand as he falls – catches the cable–

Slams hard against the back of the truck, almost loses his grip.

But not quite. He's hanging against the rear doors of the trailer. Bones steps forward.

Looks down at Shane.

And draws a knife from a sheath on his belt.

Chapter 18

Ken swerves the VW gently back and forth across the winding road to spread the smokescreen. Why is this taking so long?

"She's still coming." Mouse says.

Ken looks back over his shoulder. The truck is there, a ghost in the haze that's pouring out of the rear of the VW, headlights like the eyes of some great beast "Make the smoke thicker."

Mouse shoots him an annoyed look. "How am I supposed to–" He freezes – his eyes go wide.

Confused, Ken turns his gaze back to the road.

Ahead, an old wooden bridge crosses the river.

Or rather used to cross the river. It's missing its middle section. Sawhorses and a…

Bridge Out

…sign block the road.

Ken jams his foot on the brakes.

The VW's going too fast – it *SMASHES* the sawhorses. Wheels lock, tires *SCREAM*, leaving streaks of black on the bridge.

But the VW skids to a stop a dozen feet short of the gap. Ken and Mouse let out long sighs of relief.

DAWN

Squints into the smoke. She guides the truck by the shadows of the trees that loom periodically on either side of the road. If she stops, the Piranhaz will swarm the rig, but if she keeps going like this, she's eventually going to run off the road. Where the hell is Shane?

Two flashes of red spark in the haze ahead.

Brake lights.

She slams down her own brakes.

BONES

Crouches on the back of the trailer. Slips his knife under the cable that the trucker's clinging to. Bones is going to turn this asshole into roadkill.

SCREECH – the truck brakes suddenly, throwing Bones off balance–

He stumbles back toward the front of the trailer.

DAWN

Pushes both feet down on the brake pedal. Big rigs can't stop as fast as cars, and Dawn couldn't see very far ahead.

Creaking and groaning, the truck slows – but not quickly enough. It plows into the back of the VW hatchback at 20 mph. The *CRUNCH* of metal echoes off the canyon walls.

BONES

Is thrown off his feet by the force of the impact. He rolls farther forward on the trailer.

DAWN

Presses herself into the seat, willing the truck to stop. Slaughter whimpers from the back.

The truck slowly shoves the smaller VW toward the gap in the bridge. The front wheels of the VW slide over the edge.

The truck finally comes to a stop with a mechanical sigh.

KEN

Looks down at water roaring by twenty-five feet below. The VW teeters over the river. Its bumper is hooked into the big rig's battering ram, holding the car in place. The burning tar has spilled. The car's upholstery smolders, filling the VW with a bitter charcoal stench.

The car's bumper bends – metal *SQUEALS* – the VW angles farther down.

Mouse *moans* and sits up in back.

The VW creaks and wobbles. Ken shouts, “Don't move!”

And then the upholstery bursts into flames.

Ken and Mouse scramble to climb out of the back of the VW.

SHANE

Hangs against the back of the trailer. From the sounds of things, the truck hit something.

The Tesla skids to a stop a foot from the trailer's back armor. The woman with the shaved head behind the wheel pants in relief.

She can wait. Shane needs to deal with Bones. Shane climbs up the cable onto the roof of the trailer.

Bones is staggering to his feet at the front end of the trailer.

Shane charges–

Bones braces himself.

Shane dives – tackles Bones–

They fly off the trailer – over the fairing – slam onto the roof of the cab – tumble onto the hood of the truck. Shane stops there. Bones keeps going. Plows into two other gangsters just as they emerge from the hatchback of the VW ID.4–

The trio falls in a pile back inside the burning car.

The bumper *SQUEALS* – the VW slips farther out over the drop–

Shane looks down on Bones from the hood of his truck.

Bones meets his gaze. "You really are a bastard, you know that?"

And with that the bumper gives out.

The VW – with Bones and his two pals – plunges into the water, swallowed by the rushing river.

A moment later it bobs to the surface a hundred yards downstream.

The water must not have completely extinguished the fire, because smoke once again billows out the back. And as it floats downriver, the VW suddenly–

EXPLODES.

There is a *SCREECH* from behind the truck. Shane looks back. The Tesla pulls a U-turn, speeds away. Guess the driver decided enough is enough.

Dawn gets out of the truck on wobbly legs. Shane hops down beside her.

They hug.

"Come on," Shane says. "Let's get you back home."

Dawn leans forward as the big rig passes out of the trees, and Mt. Tucker comes into view.

The mayor and townspeople are busy repairing the town gates from the damage caused by the snowplow and the collapsed tower.

Dawn is going to be in so much trouble. They might even charge her with a crime. Hopefully nothing too serious… she's eighteen now, an adult.

Dawn's parents are there, watching the highway anxiously. Her dad points toward the truck and grabs her mom's hand.

Shane pulls the truck to a stop two dozen yards from the gate.

Dawn looks at Shane. It's hard to find the words for this moment.

"Well," Dawn says.

"Yeah," Shane replies.

“Don't be a stranger.” They bump fists.

Dawn climbs out of the truck and limps toward the gates. She hurts all over, but the ankle is the worst. Something’s grinding in there.

The mayor steps forward, blocking her entrance. “Dawn... I can't let you back in.”

Dawn’s dad turns on the mayor in shock. “What!?”

“We're a clean zone,” the mayor explains. “She left quarantine.”

“For twenty minutes!” Her dad’s hand balls into a fist.

Dawn’s father has a bad temper. He’s been known to go off on store clerks, school administrators, and government flunkies, bellowing red-faced, his veins bulging. Dawn edges forward, uses her most disarming smile. “I didn't catch anything, Mayor.”

The mayor sighs. “You know the law. The Klemper Act states that if we let you in, we lose our status and can't keep anyone out. We'll be overrun.”

“We're a small town!” her dad cries. “Who's going to know? Are you going to report her?”

“I'm sorry Joe. I can't risk the town for Dawn.”

“You bastard!” Her dad lunges at the mayor. A couple of nearby townspeople intervene, hold him back.

“Stop it, Dad!” Dawn yells.

The townspeople have pulled her dad off the mayor, but he still fumes, a
ball of clenched fury.

"It's okay," Dawn says gently. "I don't think I'd be happy in Mt. Tucker anymore anyway." As it comes out of her mouth, she realizes the truth of it.

"Dawn, no!" her mom cries. "You don't know what you're saying!"

"Yes, I do. You know I do."

"Dawn, please," her father begs.

"I love you guys."

"No!" Her mom collapses into her dad's arms.

Dawn desperately wants to hug them, but that would be a violation of quarantine rules. So, she turns and limps back to Shane, who's gotten out of the truck. "Think I could get a ride to Ashford?"

He rubs his chin. "What are you going to do there?"

"I don't know." Her decision feels right, but she's got no plan, not like she had when she ran away to meet Eric. What do regular people who live in the plague zones do? "Get a job, I guess."

Shane studies her. "You're not bad in a fight. You could work for me if you want."

A thrill runs through Dawn. "You mean, like, partners?"

"Like you work for me. And there are rules. Number one, only I drive."

"But…"

He shoots her a stern look.

"Okay, fine." She sticks out her hand. They shake on it.

They climb into the truck. Dawn waves to her weeping parents as Shane turns the truck around and heads for the interstate.

Shane guides the truck down the highway. They'll need to recharge in Ashford. He normally would have done it at Mt. Tucker, but it seemed like it would have been awkward to stick around. Taking the girl on was impulsive and probably a mistake. For starters, they're going to have to take turns sleeping in the narrow bed when they're on the road. But she has proven more resourceful than he would have guessed. It might be useful to have her around until she gets back on her feet.

Dawn interrupts his train of thought. "So, where are we going first?"

"Detroit."

"What are we hauling?"

"Nothing. I'm buying information from a guy."

"What kind of information?"

Shane exhales in frustration. "Rule number two, don't talk so much."

What's left of Bones lays face down on the muddy bank of the river. He stirs, coughs. Amazingly, he's not dead.

He rolls over. Wipes water from his eyes.

A little girl, maybe about four years old, is staring at him. She holds a teddy bear that has been "bandaged" around the midsection with duct tape.

Bones scowls. "What are *you* looking at?"

The girl licks her lips.
She's looking at dinner.

The story of Shane and Dawn's adventures will continue in future books.

Afterward

I was very fortunate to have early career success with the screenplay for *Sweet Home Alabama*, which I wrote as my Master's thesis at USC and, as you may know, became a hit movie starring Reese Witherspoon. This was a great experience and enabled me to become a full-time, professional writer. I'm extremely glad it happened. But one thing about Hollywood – and life in general – is that when you are successful at something, people want you to do the same type of thing again. I never really intended to be a romantic comedy writer. That script came from a period in my life where I was still finding my voice. What I wanted to write was fun, action-adventure movies – movies like *Aftermath*.

I originally wrote *Aftermath* as a spec screenplay to try to "change my brand" as they say in Hollywood (though the origins of the story date back to ideas I was fooling around with in college.) When I finished, I liked it so much that I didn't really want to sell it. I thought if I held onto it for a while maybe I could reach a point in my career where I could direct it. Eventually I realized the reason I was reluctant to let it go is that I wanted to create further stories about these characters, and when a writer sells a screenplay in Hollywood, they no longer have any control or ownership of that story or those characters. Typically, in fact, they are quickly removed from the project and other writers brought on board to make changes. It is not unusual for the original writer to never be consulted during the making of the actual movie. I understand and accept that collaborative process for film. But I couldn't accept it for this particular story.

I say all of this to explain why I decided to turn *Aftermath* into a novella. This will allow me to keep ownership of the underlying intellectual property and write further adventures for Shane and Dawn in prose form. Perhaps one day this will become a movie, perhaps not. But I have enjoyed writing this more than anything else I've written so far, so it's already a success for me. I hope you have also enjoyed reading it.

Many people have been instrumental in helping me grow as a writer and moving my career along and simply encouraging me in a challenging profession. Thank to you all, you know who you are. I would like to acknowledge by name some of the people that helped me out with this book and story in particular. Kevin Grange, Don Hewitt, Ron Osborn, Cindy Davis and Phillip Mottaz all were kind enough to give me feedback on various versions of the screenplay. Marilyn Thomas gave me feedback and also helped me with the Ojibway words. My sister, novelist Chris Eboch (who also writes under Kris Bock), gave me feedback on the prose and a great deal of publishing advice. I am grateful to all of you… this is a better book because of you.

About Douglas J. Eboch

Douglas J. Eboch is a professional screenwriter and director who wrote the original screenplay for the movie *Sweet Home Alabama* starring Reese Witherspoon, which set a box office record for a September opening. The screenplay began as his Master's thesis. He has co-written prequel novels about the characters from the movie, *Felony Melanie in Pageant Pandemonium*, *Felony Melanie in the Big Smashup*, and *Felony Melanie in the Great Prank War*, with his sister, Kris Bock. He wrote the novel *Totally Rad Wormhole* about two high school nerds from the 1980's who accidentally open a time portal to today and meet themselves at their high school reunion.

Doug wrote the video game *Nightmare Cove* and has sold short science fiction stories to such magazines as *The Colored Lens* and *Science Fictionery*. He wrote the non-fiction book *The Three Stages of Screenwriting*, and is the co-author, with producer Ken Aguado, of *The Hollywood Pitching Bible*.

The Scriptwriter's Network awarded Doug the Carl Sautter Screenwriting Award for Best New Voice in Feature Films. He has a BA in Film Production and an MFA in Screenwriting from the University of Southern California. He currently teaches screenwriting and pitching at LMU and Art Center College of Design.

Visit Doug's website www.douglasjeboch.com

Follow Doug on Twitter at @dougeboch

Other Fiction by Douglas J. Eboch

Totally Rad Wormhole
By Douglas J. Eboch

It's 1989, and high school seniors Alex and Roger cannot wait to graduate. High school may be heinous, but they have big plans for adulthood. Then, something goes wrong with their science project – it rips open a hole in time, a tunnel to the year 2021.

The boys journey into the future to find out how their lives will turn out. But when they meet themselves at their high school reunion, they are not pleased with what they've become and set out to change their fate.

The Teenage Adventures of Felony Melony
Based on characters from the movie
Sweet Home Alabama

Book 1: Felony Melanie in Pageant Pandemonium
By Douglas J. Eboch & Kris Bock

Book 2: Felony Melanie in the Big Smashup
By Douglas J. Eboch & Kris Bock

Introducing the new romantic comedy series featuring "Felony Melanie" seven years before the events of the movie Sweet Home Alabama.

Before Melanie Smooter became hot fashion designer Melanie Carmichael, she was known as Felony Melanie, the teenage troublemaker of Pigeon Creek, Alabama. Aching to escape the boredom of small-town life, she gets into many reckless adventures. Her boyfriend, Jake, is always by her side – and the local sheriff is usually close behind.

Non-Fiction by Douglas J. Eboch

The Three Stages of Screenwriting

By Douglas J. Eboch

A comprehensive guide to all aspects of the craft of screenwriting. This book covers the three distinct phases of creating a great screenplay – outlining, writing the first draft, and rewriting.

"It will help everyone, from novice to pro, become a better writer. And, most impressive of all, it is entertaining as hell - as engaging and fun to read as one of Doug's scripts."
-Ross LaManna ("Rush Hour")

The Hollywood Pitching Bible

By Douglas J. Eboch & Ken Aguado

"It's on my top shelf of books I can't be without."
-John Badham (Director of "Saturday Night Fever," "WarGames," "Stakeout").

Finally, a book that tells the truth about the art of pitching in Hollywood. "The Hollywood Pitching Bible" breaks it down, step by step. From choosing the right idea, to selling it in the room, this book tells you how it's done, in clear language, suitable for the beginner or the seasoned Hollywood professional.

www.ingramcontent.com/pod-product-compliance
Lightning Source LLC
LaVergne TN
LVHW050541160826
845677LV00011B/2126

* 9 7 9 8 8 4 7 8 9 7 1 9 8 *